MY FAMOUS FRENEMY

PIPER RAYNE

About My Famous Frenemy

Hollywood heartthrob, Gavin Price invaded our small town, Sunrise Bay, like he owned it.

Gavin was my biggest celebrity crush when I was young. He bears the charisma of an easygoing boy-next-door mixed with a rule-breaker personality both in person and on screen.

For a moment, I thought maybe my fairy godmother sent him to me.

Until he decided to run against my mother for mayor.

Everyone in our town knows my mom's happiness comes before my own, so I take it as my personal mission to show him who really runs this town.

I just didn't realize that being my mom's right-hand woman would put me in such close proximity to him. Very quickly, I question whether he wants to win the mayoral race or me.

my famous
FRENEMY

<u>**The Greenes**</u>

<u>**Hank's Kids**</u>
Cade Greene (34)
Co-owner Truth or Dare Brewery
Fisher Greene (32)
Sheriff
Xavier Greene (30)
Pro Football Player
Adam Greene (28)
Forest Ranger
Chevelle Greene (27)
Water Boat Tourist

<u>**Marla's Kids**</u>
Jed Greene (34)
Co-owner of Truth or Dare Brewery
Nikki Greene (31)
Radio Host
Mandi Greene (29)
Owner of SunBay Inn
Posey Greene (25)
Owner of Fringe

<u>**Hank and Marla's Kid**</u>
Rylan Greene (14)

Chapter One

Posey

From barbershops to posh salons, gossip and hair are intertwined like love and flowers.

Being a hairdresser in a small town like Sunrise Bay comes with challenges. I'm not like my sister Nikki, who loves spreading any juicy story she can on her radio segment, Scandals of Sunrise Bay. But at the same time, I can't stop people from sharing news they hear or discussing private matters while they're getting their hair done. This is especially true on Teased Thursdays, as we call them, at my salon, Fringe. Every Thursday, leisure-suit-wearing Fran and her gang of followers inundate Fringe for their weekly curl, tease, and hairspray that somehow lasts them until the following Thursday.

The difference this week is that I had no idea I'd be the topic of gossip.

"Hot Pants was down at the bay, running without a shirt again," Fran says with her eyes closed as I tower over her, washing her gray hair.

I mouth "Hot Pants?" to Malia, another hairstylist at my salon.

"Are you spying on Gavin Price again?" Malia asks, her fingers digging into Fran's biggest sidekick, Nora's, bottle-red hair.

"Fran's daughter sent us all the CDs. We've been watching that show of his," Nora says.

My eyebrows shoot up. Gavin Price, the Hollywood heartthrob who moved here permanently this past spring, is well known for his role in the teenage drama series *High Society*. I can't lie and say I didn't have pictures of him on my walls.

"I think you mean DVDs." Malia bites her lip to stop from laughing.

Fran ignores Malia's correction. "The four of us get together every Saturday night to watch two episodes. We make margaritas—virgin, of course—and eat pineapple upside-down cake."

"Sounds fun," I say, putting a towel around Fran's head and slowly raise her up in the chair so she doesn't get dizzy —a constant complaint that she posts on the Sunrise Bay social media page. As though I'm whipping people up in their chairs as though it's a carnival ride. "Let's get over to the chair now."

"He's so good-looking. You're single, Posey." She shuffles over to the chair, trying to glance back at me over her shoulder.

"Thanks for the reminder," I say, easing her down in the chair, then I gently massage the towel through her short strands.

"I just thought most of your siblings have found love. What about you?" She eyes me through the mirror.

I offer her a tight smile. She's not the first and won't be the last person who wants to discuss my love life. "Well, I have the good fortune of being the youngest. Less pressure. Lots of time still."

"Time flies."

The other two women from Fran's gang agree from the waiting area.

"The years will fly by, and sooner or later, the well of men dries up. Even here in Alaska."

It's common knowledge that the men in Alaska outnumber the women.

"You've seen all the single guys down there by the docks," I say. "They wouldn't know how to woo a woman if someone handed them roses and a box of chocolate."

Fran shakes her head at me.

"They'd probably eat the chocolate and give the roses to their mamas," Nora says in the chair next to me and chuckles.

"Malia found a good man," Fran says, grabbing Malia's hand as she passes by.

Malia kindly smiles. She knows she needs the good juju on the social media page since she cut Ginny's hair too short last week, which is why Ginny is in the waiting area and not having her hair done today.

Malia has been seeing a guy, but the relationship is new, and she's already confided to me about her concern about his lack of kindness to the waitstaff when they go out to dinner.

"Let's go back to you and the ladies watching *High Society*," I say. "I used to watch it. What season are you on?"

I want to move the conversation away from my love life. Fran is right though—lots of my siblings and stepsiblings have found the love of their lives. I'm not sure I'm ready for all that just yet anyway. I'm only twenty-four.

"We're on season three. After they graduate from high school and go on to college," Nora says. "I don't feel quite so dirty now."

Malia and I laugh, although I'm pretty sure Gavin was over eighteen in the later years he was filming *High Society*, portraying a rich teenager living in the elite circle of New York while attending a boarding school. I loved that show, but I really fell for Gavin when I was only eight and watched him in a family show called *The Carters*. He played the youngest brother, and I often imagined having a family as perfect as theirs while mine was falling apart after my dad cheated on my mom.

"I'm serious, Posey. You gotta go after him. Now that he's chosen Sunrise Bay as his home, the women are going to flock here," Fran says.

"I heard from Matt that the guys on the dock are worried he's going to steal all their women," Malia repeats what she heard from her boyfriend.

All the women agree again. Louder this time.

"He can't possibly take all the available women in this town," I say, combing out Fran's wet strands to start trimming.

"Have you been in the same room with the man? He steals all the attention. He's just got that thing, that X factor or something about him." Malia nods, as though to convince me.

I have been in the same room as him, and although yes, he does have a certain charisma with his easygoing boy-next-door vibe that's mixed with a rule-breaker, he's also the man who ran me off the road in his ridiculous Porsche rental car last summer.

Hello, we're in Alaska! Which goes to show that he's either vain or a show-off. Probably a mixture of both, which means he is *not* for me. If only I could tamp down my crush from when I was younger.

"If I was your age, Posey, I'd be showing up outside his

house in a trench coat with nothing underneath but skimpy lingerie."

I almost choke from Fran's words, smiling nicely at her through the mirror. "I'm just not like that."

Because I'm not. I never have been. I've always sat back when it comes to things involving guys, letting them come to me. Even then, trust can be hard when your dad cheated on your mom. I know there are good guys out there—my brother and stepbrothers have shown me that—but I can admit to myself that I didn't come out of my parents' divorce unscathed.

I cut Fran's hair while the entire salon dissects why Gavin Price is sticking around town, other than being good friends with my sister Nikki's husband, Logan.

Some speculate he's undercover for some important role he's trying to get into. Others say he's been chewed up and spit out by Hollywood and needs a place to hide out. Whatever the reason, Gavin has chosen this town as his home for the foreseeable future. The reason doesn't matter, because the man is so full of himself, he can go back to where he came from for all I care. Then again, I'd probably miss spotting him at The Grind or seeing him leaving Logan's gym all sweaty. It sucks having a crush on a man you don't even like.

The bell on the door rings. I don't bother looking up, putting the last roller into Fran's hair. Mostly because I've been running behind all day.

But the rush of quiet that suddenly blankets the salon makes me peek over my shoulder.

Lo and behold, Gavin Price himself stands inside, smiling at Ginny and Rita. "Hello, ladies." His voice is sultry and soothing, like a cold glass of iced tea on a hot summer day.

They both smile and whisper to one another before Rita

lifts her hand and says hi for both of them. They're like two teenage girls, I swear.

"Let's get you under the dryer," I say to Fran, and she stands from the chair.

I go to loop my arm through hers to make sure she doesn't slip on any of the hair on the floor, but she quickly shoos me away. "I'm not ninety, Posey!"

I step back and Malia shakes her head.

"Hi, Gavin, what brings you into Fringe?" Malia asks.

Isn't that my job? But I remind myself that I don't want to talk to him anyway.

"I'm here to see Posey." He smiles, and I hate the fact my stomach stirs at the sound of my name coming off his tongue.

"Oh," Fran says and stops to nudge me with her elbow.

"I heard him," I murmur. To him, I say, "Give me one minute. I have to get Fran all set."

"I can do it," she says, sitting in the chair.

"No, actually, you can't." I lower the dome over her head and turn the dryer to the correct setting.

She hits me in the stomach. "Go," she pretends to whisper when, in fact, she said it loudly enough for a smile to creep up the corners of Gavin's lips. I'm sure he's used to women fawning over him.

I walk across the salon, feeling every eye on me. It reminds me of high school when I thought it was crazy hair day, but I was a week early. I couldn't even take out all the little ponytails all over my head because I'd hair sprayed them.

"What can I help you with?" I slide behind our reception counter, picking up the pencil so I have something to do with my hands.

He runs his fingers through his unruly hair. There's a

slight wave to the texture which I can see being unmanageable if he doesn't get regular haircuts. "I hoped you might have some time to give me a cut."

"Sorry, I have Rita next, but Malia—"

"I can wait," he interjects.

Every woman makes a small sound as though he said something heart melting.

"I'm actually booked for the rest of the day, but like I was about to say—"

"He can take my appointment. You'd probably just cut mine too short like Malia did to Ginny last week." Rita fluffs up her hair.

Malia growls under her breath.

I slide to the side of Gavin to give Rita a death glare.

"Oh, I'd hate to take your appointment," Gavin says to Rita before he turns back to me. "I can just wait around and maybe you can squeeze me in at some point. I should only take ten minutes."

Again, he runs his fingers through his hair, and I can't even pretend my own fingers don't tingle with the need to thread through those strands.

Jeez, someone save me from myself.

"Ten minutes is all, huh?" Malia asks.

He turns his attention to her. She smiles softly, like the Southern girl she was born and raised to be.

"I guess I shouldn't assume. Posey?" His clear blue eyes meet mine as if he stepped off that poster from my wall when I was a kid. He's so damn hot.

I sigh. "Let's hurry. I might be able to fit in Rita as well." I usher him over to the shampoo bowl.

"I'll make this up to you, Mrs. Ashland," he says to Rita offhandedly.

"Happy to help, Gavin."

All the women giggle like preteen girls. Exactly how I would've had I met him as a child.

He leans back in the shampoo bowl, and once again, his eyes pierce into mine. A smile forms on his lips and a warm sensation runs down my body. He's too attractive for his own good.

"Are they looking?" he whispers when I bend over him to turn on the water, never more aware than at this minute how close my breasts are to my client's face when I do so.

"Um..." I glance over, and sure enough, Fran is staring at us. I nod to him.

I run the water over Gavin's hair. It's so silky, my fingers glide right through. His eyes slowly close as I massage the shampoo into his hair.

After I finish rinsing and putting a towel over his hair, his eyes pop open. "That felt amazing."

I have no idea what to say, so I say nothing. *Way to go, Posey.*

"She's good with her hands, right?" Fran interjects and ruins the moment.

I glance over to see that she's leaning with half her head outside of the dryer.

"That's what he said," Nora says from the dryer next to Fran. The two of them laugh, and a small chuckle slips out of Gavin.

I point him toward my chair, where Malia is sweeping up all of Fran and Nora's hair.

"Don't trust me, huh?" Malia asks as Gavin settles in my chair.

"Nothing like that. I just..." He looks around, seeing four sets of eyes watching his every move. "I just thought maybe Posey could do it. I didn't mean to hurt your feelings."

"Oh, believe me, I'm not that sensitive."

She clears her throat and moves her eyes toward the mirror, where Gavin is watching us with rapt attention.

"So." I turn all my focus on him. "Just a trim and a cleanup?" I run the towel over his hair and wipe my hands on it before setting it on the counter and grabbing a comb.

"Yeah, it's gotten way too long."

We discuss how much he wants trimmed off, and I set up, asking Malia to wash Rita's hair since this won't take long.

Gavin watches me work the entire time. When I'm done, he looks so much better, but our conversation was filled with superficial stuff, and I hate myself for being a little disappointed that the only reason he was looking at me was for a haircut and nothing more.

I check him out and he tips me generously, rocking back on his heels as he thanks me for the tenth time.

He lingers, so I ask, with my heart pounding, "Did you need something else?"

"No. Thanks for squeezing me in."

"That's what he said," Nora says from Malia's chair.

I groan. "Have a great day, Gavin."

He stands there for a moment, then shakes his head and leaves. The bell rings with his departure. I can't deny I feel deflated. I kinda thought maybe he was going to ask me out.

"Someone needs to get that man a set of balls," Fran breaks the silence and everyone agrees.

Chapter Two

Gavin

After living the majority of my life in Los Angeles, the small Alaskan town I've found myself in love with is the polar opposite of what I'm used to. My first trip here was supposed to be a getaway. Somewhere to escape the rumors, the gossip, the stigma of being a child star turned adult. But after returning to Los Angeles, I still found myself dreading every audition call. Hearing the same old shit—how much they loved me in *High Society* and *The Carters*, but they just couldn't see me in another role—was getting old.

I'm sure my parents never guessed that after a brief modeling career when I was six, they would end up packing up all our shit and driving across the country with all their hopes and dreams pinned on me. It only took two years before I landed *The Carters*. I was one of the lucky ones. But with my success came a lot of pressure. Pressure I didn't mind until the past couple of years.

After I leave the salon, I drive over to the neighboring town of Lake Starlight to see my good friends from Los Angeles, Griffin Thorne, and Phoenix Bailey. They've been living in both Alaska and Los Angeles for years now, but I've only ever seen them down in LA.

I'm not out of my brand-new truck for a second when Griffin steps out of the house carrying his youngest son, Jack.

"I guess when you decide to go in, you go all in. A truck?" He eyeballs my newest purchase.

He's right to question me. Back in LA, all I drove were sports cars. Anything that went fast and let me drive away from it all at top speed. Sometimes I think back to those times and think I might not have realized it, but maybe I was tempting fate, trying to harm myself. I shake the thought from my head. I've come a long way from that man-child in the past two years and I'm sure Alaska has had something to do with that.

I tap the hood of my metallic-gray Bronco. I didn't go full pickup truck, it's more SUV than anything. "I have to fit in at some point." I walk up the path toward the front door.

"Jack, you remember Gavin?" Griffin asks, trying to get the boy's attention, but he shakes his head and tightens his grip on his dad, pushing his face into his neck. "His brother won't let him play his video game."

"He took the controller out of my hands," Jack whines.

"Gavin!" Phoenix comes out of the front door. She's wearing an apron and her hair is pulled back into a ponytail. She looks like a modern-day June Cleaver.

"Is this what small-town life does to you?" I ask the woman who is known for rocking the red carpet in gorgeous gowns and heels.

"Other way around. LA life changes me. Here, I'm myself." She kisses my cheek and hugs me hello.

"It looks good on you," I murmur in her ear.

"Thanks. It looks good on you too." She steps back and appraises me. Her gaze moves up and down my jeans and cable-knit sweater. Although it's spring, it's still chilly here. At least for an LA transplant like me. "You look like you could model for *Alaska Wildlife*."

She and Griffin laugh together, and Phoenix holds her arms out for Jack. He eagerly moves into her arms, and she carries him as if he weighs five pounds.

"Come on in, I made my specialty."

"It's pot roast," Griffin murmurs. "The only thing she can cook."

"I can hear you," Phoenix calls from the family room. "And you never complain." She joins us in the kitchen sans Jack.

"Because it's my favorite." He kisses her cheek. "Anything that involves you is my favorite."

"Gross!" Maverick, Griffin's oldest son that he had with the famous actress Margaret Cooperton, comes down the stairs. I barely recognize him since I saw him last. He's so much more mature. "Pot roast? Again?"

"Until you want to make dinner for us, I don't want to hear any complaints." Phoenix holds up her spoon at him. "God, I sound just like my oldest brother, Austin. You know what? Anything you want, let me know and I'll make it." She sets down the spoon and moves to their pantry.

"No." Griffin places his hands on her shoulders and turns her around. "He'll eat what you prepare."

"Seriously, Dad?" Maverick asks, sulking when he sits at the center island.

"Call it punishment for being mean to your brother." Griffin opens the fridge, then looks over his shoulder at me. "What can I get you to drink?"

"Just a water."

Both Griffin and Phoenix smile at me. It nauseates me how much people know about my life.

"Where is the little tattletale anyway?" Maverick asks, looking around.

"I laid him on the couch, he's probably already asleep." Phoenix takes her own water from Griffin.

I'm not going to address the elephant in the room, so I pretend not to wonder if the reason neither she or Griffin are drinking is because of me.

"Good. He's a nightmare." Griffin rolls his eyes.

"He's your only brother," she says. "Have some patience."

"I took him to Sweet Suga Things yesterday for donuts." Maverick argues like the teenage boy he is.

"Was that for you or him?" Phoenix eyes him, and Maverick huffs, sliding off the stool.

"No, stay put. Say hello to Gavin Price," Griffin says. "He's moved to Sunrise Bay."

Maverick's head whips in my direction. "Why? Lake Starlight is way better."

I laugh but the kid's dead serious, so I shrug. "I like the bay."

"Well, we have a lake, and our football team kicked your team's ass this year."

"Language," Phoenix says with zero authority to her voice. Must be hard being a stepmom to a boy who towers over you.

"I don't follow much high school football, so I'm not worried about it."

"Still. Lake Starlight is way better than Sunrise Bay. Call me when dinner's ready." He disappears upstairs.

Griffin and Phoenix groan in unison.

"One day he'll remember the manners we taught him, right?" Griffin says to Phoenix. "But he is right, Lake Starlight rules and Sunrise Bay sucks."

Phoenix hits him in the stomach. "You're hanging around Jack too much."

Griffin accepts that with a nod. "Probably."

"So, did you find a place to buy?" Phoenix asks.

"Yeah, a small three-bedroom right off the bay. There's a bit of land and I can still walk into town. Once I have it rehabbed, I'll invite you guys over."

Griffin smiles. "Sounds great. Can't wait."

We discuss the new album Phoenix is putting out next fall, and she tells me a bit about her eight siblings who live in Lake Starlight. Griffin goes on and on about some new artist he's working with, emphasizing that it's confidential— as though I'd blab the information.

Out of nowhere, Phoenix changes the subject and fixes her dark eyes on me. "So what really made you move to Sunrise Bay and not Lake Starlight?"

I shrug. "I told you. Logan Stone moved there, we're buddies, so it made the most sense."

They nod, and the air in the room turns thick from their interrogation.

"I heard Logan married a Greene. My grandma hangs out with the Greenes' grandma. They're a pretty big family too." She doesn't phrase it like a question, but rather like she knows.

"Yeah, I think all in all, there are nine of them, but they're blended."

The Greene family was nice enough to invite me to their summer barbecue. Plus, I've had enough dinners with Logan and Nikki to know a bit about the family dynamic. I pay the most attention when Nikki talks about her sister Posey, who I completely blew it with earlier today.

"I think Nikki Greene has two sisters, right?" Phoenix pries.

"Yeah." I do my best to keep my voice level.

"And I think there's a younger one on Ethel's side, Chevelle, right?"

"Cool it with the inquisition, you're sounding like Dori," Griffin says.

"I'm just curious," she says and sips her water. "Could a lady be the reason you're there?"

Never in a million years would I lay my cards out for Phoenix. She's too close and would probably try to fix me up. Logan already warned me about Ethel and her friend Dori, how manipulating they can be. Said to watch myself if I don't want to be fixed up with a Greene because they'll sway me that way. He also doesn't want me to fuck anything up with him and Nikki. He has good reason to be worried. I've never had a real relationship. I tend to keep people at arm's length.

I need to change this conversation. "You want to know a secret?"

They both lean forward. Is this what small-town life does? You become eager for gossip?

"I'm going to run for mayor," I say. "Rumor is that the current mayor ran off with his mistress, so the position is up for grabs. I put in my name this morning."

Their eyebrows shoot up to their hairlines.

"What?" My forehead wrinkles.

"Okay, Arnold Schwarzenegger." Griffin laughs. "What the hell?"

I shrug because I don't really have a specific reason why I decided to try to enter politics. It felt right and I want to do anything besides acting in this moment.

Phoenix touches my hand. "Gav, I hate to break it to you, but if you want to keep skeletons *in* your closet, running to be the mayor of a small town isn't gonna keep them there. You think LA is ruthless? Just wait. It'll all come out."

"You know as well as I do that nothing about my life has ever stayed hidden. Maybe the news hasn't traveled up here yet, but it's in print and online. I know that."

She bites her lower lip, looking as concerned as if I were her naive baby boy who just enlisted in the military—which gives me pause for a second. Maybe I shouldn't have put my name in for mayor.

"But on another subject," I say because I don't want them to talk me out of it. "There is a girl I was too chicken-shit to ask out an hour ago."

Phoenix slaps the counter. "I knew it. Is the mayor thing a joke?"

"No, I'm honestly going out for Sunrise Bay mayor."

"Who's the girl?" Griffin asks.

"She's a Greene. Posey."

Phoenix grins. "Owns Fringe?"

I nod.

"It looked like you just got a haircut," Griffin says. "How were you chickenshit?"

I go to run my fingers through my hair before remembering there's gel in it. For a moment, I remember the feel of her hands through my hair while she leaned over me, her breast brushing against my arm. "I went there to ask her to dinner, but all the other women there were listening to us."

"That happens," Phoenix says. "You need to realize two things. In Lake Starlight, we have Buzz Wheel that spreads the gossip around every day, but Sunrise Bay has *Scandals of Sunrise Bay*, a radio show that airs anything Nikki Greene sniffs out. So, watch yourself."

The buzzer for the oven goes off and she turns around to attend to it.

"Doesn't matter. I totally messed it up."

"Why not go back there when the salon is closing?" Griffin asks.

I look at the clock. Fringe doesn't close for another two hours. "That's not a bad idea. I'm not sure she likes me, so I want to do it when no one's around."

We chat a while longer, and when I sit at the table to eat with their family, I hear about schools, colleges, and all of Phoenix's nieces and nephews. I help clean the dishes while Griffin reprimands Maverick for his choice of language at the table.

"Let's go outside," Griffin says to me after he's done his parenting duty. "Phoenix, you got this?"

"Uh-huh," she says and shakes her head. "Mav will help me."

He groans but stays at his stepmother's side, helping her with the dishes.

We go back outside, and Griffin slaps me on the back. "Let me give you one piece of advice when it comes to the women around here."

"You're talking as if they're another species."

He doesn't laugh. "There's a lot of competition in Alaska, numbers being what they are. And your name means jack shit around here."

I want to call bullshit, because I see the way Posey looks at me. It's one reason I was going to stay away from her. I don't want someone who's into me because of my celebrity status.

At least she used to look at me like I hung the moon. As though she'd been praying for me to come alive off whatever picture she had of me hanging on her wall. But ever since the unfortunate incident of me almost running her over, there's been an undercurrent of distrust and hatred, and

God help me, I like that.

"Meaning?"

"Get your ass in your truck and go ask her out. And do it properly this time."

I chuckle, but he's dead serious, so I do exactly that.

Chapter Three

Posey

"Hot date with Matt tonight?" I ask Malia, locking the front door of Fringe.

"He's coming over. I told him I would cook." She sets her purse on the ground and puts on her jacket. "It's colder than I thought."

"I hope he treats you better than he does the servers." I shove my keys in my purse.

"I only agreed because I want to see how he handles himself. This could be the end or a new beginning. It'll depend on how he treats me." She looks over my shoulder and purses her lips. "I better get going."

"Oh. Okay," I say, swinging my bag over my shoulder.

"See you tomorrow." She leans to the side of me and lifts her hand in a wave. "Hi, Gavin."

"Hi, Malia." That deep voice sends a shiver up my spine.

Malia giggles as though she can tell the effect he has on me and turns around, heading to the parking lot.

Slowly, I circle to come face-to-face with Gavin. He's still wearing his jeans and cable knit sweater, and his model good looks and smile throw me off-kilter. "Hi."

He shoves his hands in his pockets and glances around the square that's busier over by the brewery. What's his deal? Did he forget something in the salon?

"Hey, Posey." His eyes find mine and don't veer away. "I'd wanted to ask you earlier..."

"Yeah, I'm sorry. Fran and her gang take gossiping to a whole other level." He opens his mouth, but I ramble on. "If you want to schedule something more private next time..." Wait, what am I saying? "What I mean is—"

He chuckles. "Do you want to go out with me?"

My eyes widen and I swear I don't breathe for a full minute. "What?"

"Dinner? A walk? Coffee? Whatever you're comfortable with."

I blink and blink again. Yep. It's Gavin Price standing in front of me, saying these words.

"But..."

He steps forward. "Let me apologize for running you off the road. Show you I'm not all bad."

"Oh," I say, realization dawning. This isn't about wooing me. It's about me forgiving him. Well, I don't need his pity. "It's fine." I pull my red hair off my forehead where there's the lightest scar as a result of my injury from the incident in question. "All healed up."

"Still. I'd like to make it up to you." From his eyes, he seems earnest. Something I've never really noticed until now. But I'm not a pity case to anyone.

"Honestly, Gavin, it's very thoughtful, but not necessary. It was nice running into you, see you around." I move to walk around him, and he stretches out his arm to grab mine.

I stop, mostly from the rush of tingles racing up my arm to disperse throughout my body.

"I want to. Maybe I'm not saying this right."

I pull my arm from his hand, and he sighs. "Gavi—"

"Posey, go on a date with me. Not as an apology for driving you off the road, although I am sorry about that. But

I like you and I want to go on a date with you to get to know you better."

He stumbles through as though this is his first time asking a woman out. Then again, it might be. He's probably used to women in the lower forty-eight throwing themselves at him.

"Um..."

"I know I'm not your favorite person, but all I'm asking for is a few hours. Or even one hour. No time requirement necessary." His cheeks turn the slightest shade of pink and it's so adorable. So opposite of the confident guy he played in *High Society*.

Here I thought he'd be all suave and cavalier, but he's adorably fumbling through this entire exchange.

"So, five minutes would work?" I cross my arms.

His eyebrows scrunch for a moment, but he straightens them. "Yeah. Sure."

I laugh and touch him because that's the kind of person I am. Touchy. To a fault. His gaze diverts quickly to my hand and back to my eyes. "I never pegged you for a shy guy."

I can just hear my sister, Mandi, in my head. "If you want the guy to ask you out, don't call him out."

But do I want him to ask me out? Kind of. I mean, yeah, he ran me off the road, but that was almost a year ago.

"I can tell you for certain, I've never been this nervous to ask out a woman before." He rocks back on his heels, peeking at me.

"Why? You're Gavin Price."

He rolls his eyes. "I'm still a guy, Posey."

"Sure, but I have to be one of many." I hike my bag farther up on my shoulder.

He huffs.

"You know what? This is—"

Before I can finish, he presses two fingers to my lips. "I'm nervous because you're different. Because you're Posey Greene and you're headstrong and don't give a shit that I'm Gavin Price."

My thoughts are traveling at warp speed as I try to make sense of what he just said. I attempt to open my mouth despite his fingers, but he's quick to cut me off.

"Go out with me? Tomorrow night. We'll have dinner. I'll pick you up at five." He lowers his fingers but doesn't step away.

My body feels as though it's made of goo. I'm not sure if I can stand up straight after his declaration. "I'd love to." The truth comes out of my mouth before I can decide whether it's a good idea or not.

"Great, now I'll walk you to your car."

I chuckle.

"What?" His forehead scrunches up in the same way I remember it doing on *The Carters* when he was acting confused.

"It's okay, I'm going to my sister's inn right now."

Although that wasn't my original plan, it is now that he's asked me out. She's the only Greene besides Chevelle who would understand how huge this is.

"I can walk you there then." He glances around. "It's getting dark."

"It's Sunrise Bay. I'll be fine, but thank you for the concern."

"It would make me feel better if you'd let me walk you." He fixes his blue gaze on me.

"Suit yourself."

We fall in line down the cobblestone street of our little downtown area. We pass by the brewery, where we catch the attention of patrons downing their beer.

"I really am sorry about running you off the road last year."

"Just think, now I'll always remember you." I motion to the small scar on my forehead.

He winces. "I'm not sure that's a good thing."

I shrug. "It's a physical scar. I think emotional scars are much worse."

"That's the truth. I always felt like I'd rather be pummeled to death in the ring by Logan than read another tell-all article about myself."

We stop in the parking lot of the inn. Mandi's got a great location here, so close to downtown and right on the bay.

"I can't imagine living in the limelight," I say. "I mean, being a Greene in this town is no easy feat, but you have the entire world watching you."

"It sucked, to be honest. If I ever want to see how bad those awkward teenage years were for me, all I have to do is Google myself." He laughs.

"I don't remember any awkward years," I admit.

He places his hand on my forearm before we enter the inn. I stop and look up at him. He's obviously contemplating something, though he doesn't say anything at first.

"Tomorrow night, can we please not talk about *High Society* or *The Carters* or any of that shit? Can we just be a normal couple on a date?"

I nod, seeing in his eyes how important it is. "So, no fawning over the Hollywood heartthrob? I can't ask you for all the dish?" I give him an exaggerated pout.

He smiles, but there's a tinge of sadness to it. "Yeah."

"I think I can do that."

"Good." His chest rises and falls with a deep breath as his gaze flickers from the inn back to me.

When our eyes meet, it feels impossible to look away.

The surge of electricity between us isn't anything I've ever felt before.

If I'm honest, the reason I put so much effort into hating him after he ran me off the road was because that pull to him scares me. He was a drifter then. A guy who rented sports cars and spent a few weeks here sometimes. Definitely couldn't be trusted with a lifestyle like that. But now he's a Sunrise Bay resident. Maybe things can be different.

"Have you gotten your driver's license for Alaska yet?"

He narrows his eyes. "Yeah."

"Can I see it?"

Without asking any questions, he reaches back in his pocket and hands me the piece of plastic.

"This is your address?" I ask, reading the street I already know he bought a house on. News travels fast here. He's bought a house, got his state driver's license, and changed the address on his ID. He must be serious about sticking around and not using his place here as a vacation getaway.

"Yep."

I hand him back the license. "So you're really doing this small-town thing, huh?"

"I really am. I even decided earlier today—"

"*Posey*!"

We both look to our right. An old high school friend, Maggie, is just coming out of the inn with what will be her fifth boyfriend this year. She moves fast, constantly looking for her happily ever after. But who am I to judge? I move like a tortoise toward love.

"You didn't tell me you knew Gavin Price!" she says.

I mouth *sorry* to Gavin before she weaves her way over with her boyfriend, who I think is from Greywall. I'm assuming she's had too much to drink from the way he's helping her keep standing.

"Keeping this one all hidden, huh?" She extends her arm for a handshake. "I'm Maggie."

"Hi, Maggie," he says, without introducing himself.

I've never thought about the fact that Gavin doesn't have to tell people his name. More than likely, they already know it. I can't imagine what it's like to just walk around and have people know not only who you are, but all about your life.

"Oh, you're all grown up." She leans forward. "I used to masturbate to your picture on my wall." She brings two fingers close to his eyes. "With those eyes staring back at me."

I have to choke back a cough, but Gavin seems nonplussed, as though he hears this stuff all the time.

The boyfriend chuckles and I give him a look to shut up. He ignores my look and I see that poor Maggie will have to find a sixth boyfriend by the time the year's done because this guy will never last.

"I fucking loved you in *High Society*. You were such an asshole," he says.

Gavin forces a smile. "Well, that's just the role. Not really me."

"Yeah, but to be that big of a dick, you must have it in you," the guy continues.

Meanwhile, Maggie's gaze is roving all over Gavin as though he's her prize at an auction. No doubt thinking of all the things she'd do to him.

"Not really. It's called acting." Gavin's jaw tenses and his eyes meet mine. "You good?"

I nod. "Yeah. Go."

"No one is that good of an actor, dude," the guy says.

Gavin doesn't even respond, turning his back to us and walking back into town.

"See, that's a dick move. I was right." Maggie's date looks at me.

I roll my eyes.

"Are you fucking him? How lucky are you?" Her words slur and I'm wondering how she got so drunk at the inn.

"No, I'm not. Have a great night. Get her home safely," I tell the guy.

"You need new friends, Mag," the guy says when I walk away, and he leads her to the car.

I refrain from saying I'm not her friend and Gavin, for sure, isn't her friend.

I walk into the inn and find Mandi at a table by the hostess stand, folding up silverware.

I slide into the booth on the other side of her. "Did you overserve Maggie Mitchell?"

Mandi scoffs. "No, she and that twat were drinking down at the beach. She just came in here to use the bathroom."

"That makes more sense. Guess what?" I lean back in the booth.

Her eyebrows rise. "It's been a bad day, just tell me."

"Come on. Guess," I whine like we're kids again.

"Gavin Price asked you out," she says matter-of-factly.

My hand slams on the table. "How did you know?"

She laughs. "He did it in the middle of downtown during tourist season. Did you think the news wouldn't travel fast?"

She slides her cell phone over to me. I open it and see a picture of us outside Fringe a few minutes ago, Gavin's fingers pressed to my lips.

"What the hell?"

"It's Fran, I think. She's turning what should be our social media group about things regarding the town into a gossip blog."

"Is she trying to be Lake Starlight Buzz Wheel?" The

neighboring town has a blog that posts the latest gossip every day, then it disappears at midnight.

Mandi shrugs. "I don't know, but you two have been outed." She continues to fold the silverware into the napkins. "Now tell me what you're going to wear."

All that excitement I felt moments ago resurfaces.

Just as I'm about to gush over everything that happened, a whirl of blonde hair flies into the small restaurant attached to Mandi's inn. "O-M-G, you're going out with Gavin Price!" Chevelle slides in next to me. "Give me all the deets!"

God, I love these two.

Chapter Four

Posey

"UGH!" I scream and toss the curling wand on the bathroom counter. I know I'm a hairstylist, but believe me when I tell you that after doing everyone else's hair for eight hours a day, doing my own holds no appeal. Especially when it's not cooperating.

"What's up?" Chevelle comes in and sits on the toilet seat. She puts her hands together in giddy excitement. "Just think back to your sixteen-year-old self. You're going out with Blake Michaels." She feigns passing out with the back of her hand on her forehead. True drama, but that's kind of my stepsister's style.

"I'm going out with Gavin Price."

"Same thing." She sits up straighter and watches me.

"Here, let me." Mandi walks into the already small space and takes the curling wand from the counter. She's a great big sister. Now that we're older.

"It's not the same thing, Chevelle. I'm starting to think he doesn't like to talk about being a childhood star."

"Who would?" Mandi says. "I would never be able to be ridiculed like that in a public forum."

Chevelle raises her hand. "I would. I mean, not the whole ridiculed thing, but the fame and stuff."

"Only you," Mandi says and shakes her head.

"Not only me. Obviously there are a lot of actors and actresses out there who love what they do. The media is the con to a heavy list of pros."

I stand as still as I can for Mandi. "To each their own, but he did ask me not to talk about his time on *High Society* and *The Carters* tonight."

"So, it's open game to talk about that war movie of his that flopped?" Chevelle asks, crossing her legs and pointing at my hair. "Redo that one strand." Mandi shoots her an annoyed glare and Chevelle laughs, holding up her hands. "If you're gonna do a job, do it right."

"Okay, Hank," Mandi says.

"Sue me for being raised by the man." She shrugs, unaffected.

"We were raised by him too," I say.

Chevelle and her four brothers are Hank's biological children. Mandi, Nikki, our brother Jed, and I are my mom's. We blended into a new version of family when I was nine.

"I've been hearing it since birth," Chevelle says.

"Where is he taking you?" Mandi asks, finishing the last strand of hair.

"I don't know. He just said he'd pick me up at five."

"You message us the minute you get somewhere," Chevelle says. "You never know."

"I thought you were just saying how cool it must be to be him." Mandi sprays my hair, putting her fingers through my long red strands.

"Yeah, but I'm not naive. Maybe he came to Sunrise Bay because the LAPD is closing in on him."

"Closing in on him?" I don't know why I bother leading Chevelle down this road.

Her eyes go wide. "They discovered where he hid the bodies."

"Bodies?" Mandi's forehead is wrinkled in confusion.

"Of the ones he lured in with those good looks and actor charisma, only to bury them alive."

We both stare at her in awe.

"Do I need to take you to the hospital?" Mandi asks.

Chevelle waves us off. "I'm just saying. Did I tell you about this creepy guy I keep seeing at the docks?"

"Do we want to know?" Mandi asks.

"He's going out late at night. The other day I had an early morning gig with these salespeople from Seattle and he was just returning," Chevelle says.

"So?" Mandi asks.

"Night fishing? Come on. He's totally dropping bodies in the water. I told Cam."

"And what did he say?" I ask.

Cam is Cameron Baker, heir to Baker Enterprises, which owns all of the fishing docks. He's also my stepbrother, Fisher's best friend.

"He said we should scope him out and follow him one night." She gives a full-body shiver.

"Are you going to?" Mandi asks.

"*No!*" she screeches. "Me on a boat with Cam and no witnesses in the dead of night? One of us wouldn't be coming back."

Mandi and I laugh. Chevelle and Cam have a sibling-like relationship, except there's an undercurrent of something else that the rest of us are trying to figure out.

"Hello!" we hear from downstairs.

We all look at one another.

Mom.

"Shit, my room." Chevelle flies out of the bathroom, accidentally knocking Mandi with her shoulder. Her bedroom door slams a second later.

"We're up here," I yell.

Mandi's not concerned because she's a neat freak. Mom is a bit of a pill when it comes to us having a clean house. Now that it's only Fisher and Allie living with their twins in the old Greene family home and the former bachelor pad is no longer, she's been harping on us.

I walk out of the bathroom and into my room to get changed for tonight.

"Where are you going?" my mom asks as she comes in. She's wearing jeans and a cardigan, and I see my stepbrother Xavier right behind her.

"I'm going on a date."

Chevelle's door opens. "With Gavin Price!" She slams it shut.

"I thought he ran you off the road?" Xavier asks.

"That was a year ago. You should know as well as anyone that a lot changes in a year." I eye him because ever since he signed the biggest deal for a professional football player in league history, he's done a one-eighty. Dating models and dressing up. Acting as though he's too good for this town. "I'm actually surprised to see you in town."

Xavier has returned every year for off-season. He used to spend the majority of that time with his best friend, Clara. But the two of them are on the outs and every Greene family member wants to know what the hell happened. She used to be his biggest supporter and now they don't even talk.

"I'm only here for the weekend. Head back in two days."

"And you're staying at your house?" I ask.

Chevelle's door opens. "Clara dyed her hair!" The door slams again and all we can hear is drawers shutting and movement behind the door.

"Marla, can we get on with this?" Xavier disregards

Chevelle's comment about Clara dying her hair completely blonde.

"So as you know, I'm campaigning for mayor," Marla says to us.

"Campaigning?" Mandi asks.

"Yes, someone else has put their name in, so looks like I'll have an opponent." She sighs and I narrow my eyes.

"Who?" I ask. My poor mom has been through the wringer with this mayor stuff.

Mom shrugs.

Xavier pulls a Vote Greene pin from the box he's holding and passes it to Mandi.

A couple years ago, she lost the campaign to our incumbent mayor, Sam Klein. Then she took over when he fled with his mistress last year, and now, she has to run to win the spot officially. I know it's something she really wants.

"They aren't telling me. Said everyone has until a certain date to put in their nomination, then they'll make a big announcement."

"But—" Mandi starts.

Mom is quick to cut her off. "That's all I know. Believe me, Nikki is trying to find out who else wants to be mayor, but no one has owned up to it at this point."

Her disappointment is evident in her eyes. I think about her loss the first time and my chest feels tight. I am not going to let my mom lose again.

"What do you need me to do?" There's steel in my voice.

"You're busy, Posey. I've got it."

Chevelle's door opens. "You got this, Marla!" She slams it again.

"Honestly, Mom, things are calm at Fringe. I could use a distraction. I'll totally be your campaign manager."

Mom shakes her head. "I can't ask that of you."

"You're not asking. I'm volunteering." I snap my fingers and hold out my palm. "Give me a pin, Xavier."

He groans. "How do I go from never waiting in a line at a club or restaurant to passing out fucking pins?"

Mandi smacks him in the back of the head. "Language."

He rubs where she hit him.

"So?" I ask Mom.

She pretends to think it over.

Chevelle's door opens. "You know she's going to do it anyway, so just agree." She slams it again.

A smile creeps across my mom's lips. "Are you sure?"

"Definitely," I say with a smile.

"Okay. You're my campaign manager."

Xavier crosses the small hallway we're all huddled in and shoves the box in my arms. "Then these are for you. I'm out."

He walks down the stairs without another word. For a moment, we all share a concerned look, having no idea what's going on with him.

"Yay!" I say to break the tension, and I give my mom a huge hug.

Mandi joins in and we're all jumping and screaming in excitement.

"Aw..." Chevelle whines from the other side of the door.

"Chevelle, I know your room is messy, just come out here," my mom says, and her door springs open.

Chevelle flies down the hallway and joins our hug. "Marla Greene for mayor!"

We're interrupted by the doorbell ringing and I look down at myself to see that I'm still wearing jogging pants and a T-shirt. "Crap. I gotta get dressed."

"I'll distract him," Chevelle says and beelines down the stairs.

"Don't drill him!" I yell after her, but we both know she will.

"I'll go keep an eye on her." Mandi follows her down the stairs.

"I'll help you," Mom says to me.

My mom and I go back into my room, where we disagree on what I should wear. She wants me in the dress I wore on Easter, but I opt to ditch the flowers and go with a black flowy skirt that has a slit up the side, paired with a burgundy blouse that plummets between my breasts. It's not too revealing, but enough to entice. Or at least, I hope it is.

I carry my heels so I won't trip down the stairs like that one teen movie that Gavin probably knows the actors from.

"So, were you really best friends with Trey Doyle?" Chevelle asks as I enter the room.

Gavin is in the recliner and she's as close to him as she can get on the couch, leaned over her crossed legs. "We were friends. Yes."

"And what about Mackenzie? Did you date her?"

Gavin catches me in his peripheral vision and my stomach somersaults when the corners of his lips tip into a wide smile. "Hey," he says, standing.

"Hi." I wave like an idiot.

There's no way this thing between us can be as powerful as it feels.

"Hi, Gavin." Mom steps out from behind me.

"Mrs. Greene. Nice to see you again." They shake hands.

"You as well. I heard you're a permanent resident of Sunrise Bay now?" Mom asks.

He tears his gaze away from me but keeps glancing in my direction as though he's afraid I might flee. "Bought a house down the road from Logan and Nikki."

"That's wonderful. Welcome to town." Mom smiles warmly at him.

"As a new resident, here's a pin for who you're voting for." Chevelle digs into her pocket and steps up to Gavin, pinning the Vote Greene button to his shirt.

He stares at it for a moment and something like discomfort passes over his features.

"You don't have to wear that," I say quickly. "Chevelle, take it off."

"Why? He's good for at least Fran and her gang's votes. They follow him around like he'll lead them to the fountain of youth."

"Truth," Mandi chimes in.

"Ready?" Gavin asks, his mood suddenly shifting. I can't blame him. I've wanted to get out of my family's presence many times before.

"Yeah."

Mom opens the front door, and there are Hank and Rylan.

"Hey, just came by to see who wants to go to dinner?" Hank says. "But I see..." His eyes set on Gavin. He waves his finger between us as if he's not happy about it. "I heard about this."

"Yeah, and we have to go," I say.

"It's nice to see you again, Mr. Greene." Gavin put out his hand.

Hank shakes it. "You gonna manage to not run anyone over tonight? Should I keep Rylan home?"

Oh seriously, we are not having this protective dad speech, are we?

"He's wearing a Vote Greene pin, let it go." I slide my arm through Gavin's, urging us to step away, but his feet don't move.

"I promise you, Mr. Greene, that was a one-time incident and I plan to make up for it tonight." Gavin looks at me and a shiver runs up my spine.

"That a boy, Gavin!" Chevelle slaps him on the back, her purse already across her body. She swings her arm around Rylan's shoulders. "Come on, Ry Guy! Break any more laws lately?"

He groans and lets his head fall back.

"Have fun, you two," Mom says and gently tugs on Hank's arm.

Eventually he turns back around, and Mandi joins them as they walk up the hill toward my family's house.

"I'm so sorry," I whisper.

"Don't be. My family is much worse." Gavin walks us to the Bronco he bought and opens the door for me.

I haven't been on a date in a long time, but this feels right.

Once he's in the driver's seat and situated, I ask, "Where are we going?"

"It's a surprise."

Then he backs out of the driveway, and we head toward the docks.

I smile. It's like all my childhood fantasies are coming true.

Chapter Five

Gavin

My mind is blank as we drive toward the docks. I'm wearing a fucking Vote Greene pin and I'm running for mayor myself. I guess I thought Marla was just filling in until the election. I didn't think she'd want to run herself. From what I can tell, most of her time is spent with her grandchildren.

How did it not cross my mind I could be running against Posey's mom? A Greene, nonetheless. Might as well torch my new house right now.

"Are you sure you want to do this?" Posey asks from next to me. The skirt she's wearing is open enough to show me her luscious, long legs. The woman is gorgeous.

I turn to her briefly before looking back at the road. "Yeah. Definitely."

"If your mood shift is about my family, I could lie and say they aren't like that, but they are."

I glance at her one more time and see she's biting the corner of her lip. Instinctively, I touch her thigh to give it a reassuring squeeze. She moves her leg away and my hand drops to the center console. Seriously, I'm an idiot.

"Sorry..." I pause, unsure what to say but happy we've arrived at the boat docks. Maybe I can figure out a new game plan for wooing Posey. "I was just going to say, don't worry about it. I like your family. Even more than my own."

She's quick to grab the door handle, and as I exit the truck, I try to get myself together. I'm Gavin fucking Price. Most women would love to go out with me. I've had everything from A-list actresses to top music performers. But Posey Greene, a small-town hair salon owner, makes me tongue-tied? I shake my head at myself.

"Should I be concerned you're going to toss me overboard?" she says, the two of us walking down the wooden docks. "Just so you know, I'm texting my sisters so they know where we are." Her thumbs move across the screen of her phone. "And I'm not sure if you know this, but the owner of the fishing docks, the Bakers, their son Cameron is my brother's best friend."

I chuckle, but it's clear she doesn't find it as funny as I do. "Yeah, I know Cameron. He helped me plan tonight."

She stops walking and stares at me. "He did?"

I nod. "Did you forget that I was at your family's summer bash?"

"Of course I remember. That's when I got this lovely little scar." She points at her head. I could kick myself for ever being so lost in my own head that I didn't see her.

"Well, Cam and I met even before that. Logan and Cam and Fisher flew down to Los Angeles once to watch Xavier play an away game. We all hung out."

"You hung out with my stepbrothers? And they never said anything?" She looks surprised.

"More Cam than Fisher, because I'm not sure if you know this, but Fisher is a hard guy to get on his good side."

She giggles. "He's the sheriff and keeps his emotions close to his chest. Plus, he's protective and he might hold the whole you running me off the road thing against you."

"I have a feeling that's going to be on my tombstone. 'Gavin Price. Shitty son. Shitty actor. Drove Posey Greene off the road once. May he rest in peace.'"

"Shitty son?"

I shake my head, not wanting to dive into my childhood crap right now. It's bad enough that in about ten minutes, I'll be telling her I'm running against her mom to be mayor. I don't need to add mommy and daddy drama on top of that.

"There's our boat." I point toward the large vessel that's lit up as though we're filming this on television. I'm gonna have to pay Cam back big time for this one.

"Gavin," she says, her mouth slightly ajar. It's the effect I wanted, but I fear I'm raising her expectations. If she agrees to a second date, how will I ever top this? "This is..."

Cam comes down from the office buildings in front of the pier. "Hey, you two." His gaze shifts from me to the boat and back to me. "Nice, right? I told you I have connections." He places his hand on my shoulder.

"Seems you do. Thanks."

"Cam, what the hell? Who did you bribe to get a boat like this to come here?" Posey sighs and walks toward it.

"We get affluent people up here too."

She gives him a bored stare and shakes her head. "You might be able to fool him." She thumbs in my direction. "But you can't fool me. Tell me you're not selling drugs or something."

My eyebrows shoot up. Why would she assume that? The last thing my reputation needs right now is to be tied to a dealer.

"Shit, Posey, you think I'd get involved in that? Fisher's my best friend—he'd kill me before the cartel had a chance." Cam walks with us. "It's a friend of my dad's. He travels up here as soon as the weather breaks. Big fisherman. They had their son's wedding, so they docked here for a bit before they fly back. When I mentioned this was for Gavin Price, he was more than willing to let us use it. There's just the one thing..." He eyes me. "That thing we talked about."

"What's that?" Posey reaches the front of the boat and turns around to face us.

Cam puts out his hand. I groan and pass him my phone.

"What's going on?" Posey asks.

Cam walks back a ways.

"Why don't you go stand with Cam? You shouldn't be in the picture," I say to her.

She gets a sour look on her face. Might as well chalk those words up to another fucked-up thing I did on this date. Who knew dating in a small town is so difficult? Most women in Los Angeles knew the deal if I asked them to step aside for a picture to be taken.

"Let's make it fast."

"You got it." Cam positions the camera and I hear Posey whispering to him, but I can't hear what they're saying from the breeze and the sound of a fishing boat five docks over. "Ready?"

"Yeah."

I plaster on the fake-ass smile I perfected more than a decade ago and bring one hand up to cup the back of my neck so that my arm now covers Marla's pin. Cam takes a few pictures, then he and Posey walk back over to me.

He hands me my phone. "You can pick the best one, just make sure you tag the business."

I nod and pocket my phone. "Got it. Thanks again, Cam." I put out my hand, and he shakes it.

"Now that that's out of the way, I do feel like I need to

give you a disclaimer," he says. "Mess with Posey and I will have to kick your ass on the principle that she's a Greene and kind of like my little sister."

"Oh please," Posey says and takes my shoulder, turning me toward the boat. "Bye, Cam, you've crashed my date enough already."

"You two kids have fun!" Cam shouts.

Posey slips off her heels once we board, and I notice her cute green polished toenails. I find it endearing that she doesn't wear the typical pink or red.

The captain and a few service people are waiting for us with glasses of champagne. I politely accept mine, but don't sip it. They show us around and the captain tells us that we'll be leaving the port shortly and to enjoy the view on the way. Dinner will be served once we're on open water.

"This is way too much. What did you have to agree to?" Posey asks.

I wait for her to sit on the cushions toward the front of the boat, then I join her. "Just to show off that it's his boat and tag him on my social media."

"Amazing what fame can bring you," she says.

The server, Serena, comes over and I hand her my champagne, asking for a water with the top still sealed. Posey asks for a white wine and Serena disappears back to the inside.

"You don't drink?" she asks. Of course, she probably already knows. Although it was rumored that I went to rehab, no one found actual proof, but people aren't stupid.

"I've been sober for about two years."

Her eyes widen. "I didn't know that. How did you hide that from the press?"

I shrug. "My manager said that one day it would give me

an edge—a feel-good story about the kid who got his shit together and made himself a star again—so he squashed the press at the time. But I guess there's too many of us now, so it's not interesting."

"It must be hard," she says, genuine concern in her tone.

I shrug. "Everything has its pros and cons."

She doesn't say anything but turns to stare out at the water. Her red hair flows in the wind. "This really is amazing. Thank you, Gavin."

"I should be thanking you for joining me."

Her gaze falls to me, and she chuckles. "Oh jeez, I forgot you had this." Reaching forward, she takes the pin off my sweater. "You have my mom's pin on you still." She sets it between us on the leather couch. "She'll love that you wore it in a picture."

Guess she didn't notice how I strategically covered it. That only makes my guilt feel heavier.

"About your mom running for mayor..." I broach the subject that I should've mentioned earlier—before I allowed them to put a pin on me that endorses another candidate.

"It's something she's always wanted. You know she ran against Sam Klein before he got reelected? I've never seen her so happy as when she was able to step into the role after Sam vacated his post."

Serena returns and hands us our drinks. Posey thanks her, but quickly goes back to talking about her mom with so much enthusiasm that jealousy coils inside me because of the horrible relationship I have with my own mother.

"You'll find this out if you don't know already, but my dad cheated on my mom, which is when we moved here. She fell in love with Hank, who is my dad's cousin." Posey flings her hand like, who cares about that. "But before she met Hank, she was always so sad. Always crying but trying to act like she wasn't. She never worked when she was married to my dad—he forbade it when we were younger. She's constantly telling us to make sure we have our own goals separate from any partners we might have." She sips her wine, and I open my mouth to use the break so I can come clean about running against her mom for mayor, but she keeps going before I can get the words out. "So she has her goal now, and I agreed to be her campaign manager." She cringes as though she's nervous, but it's clear that her excitement is through the roof.

"That's great." I feign enthusiasm. This is one of those times being an actor pays off, because she doesn't seem to notice that anything is off with me.

I'm not sure how I move on from here. *Great that you're her campaign manager, but I'm running for mayor too.*

"There's so much that needs to happen in Sunrise Bay. More tourism for sure. The schools need more supplies to catch up to the other areas. Have you looked at the cobblestone downtown? One day someone is gonna trip and fall. Sam Klein was all ego and no action. I know my mom will make the changes needed." She sips her wine and sort of cringes. "I'm sorry. I'm just excited. She's sacrificed so much for our family all these years and now that Rylan is fourteen, it's her time to do something for herself. I love that I get to be part of it with her. To know that maybe I helped her a little bit since she's done so much for me."

"That's exciting for sure. Good luck to her and you." I raise my water and Posey pretends to clink her glass with the bottle.

"Enough about me, tell me about you. I don't like that you said shitty son earlier. Is the first date too early for me to dig into your issues?" She chuckles.

I like that she's a talker and so open about who she is. It's a welcome change from the women in LA, who are so eager to morph into whoever they think I want them to be. I don't want to sink this ship before it's sailed, so I decide that I'll tell her as soon as we're back on land.

Chapter Six

Posey

Gavin's body tenses at my request to find out more about him. He was clear earlier that he didn't want me to talk about his acting, but this is a first date and I've already rambled on enough. I want to know more about him and he's the one who mentioned not being a good son.

"I don't call or visit enough. I don't take the roles they think I should." He gulps down some of his water. "My mom guilt-trips me."

"Where do they live?"

"They're back in California. Probably will never leave."

"And you're an only child?"

He nods, sipping his water again, clearly uncomfortable talking about his parents.

I touch his arm. He doesn't retract like I did in the truck. "I want you to know that I'm not going to tell anyone anything you tell me. I'm not a gossipy person. You can trust me."

"Thanks. But it's not that. There isn't much about me that isn't printed in a magazine or spread around the Internet. You could probably find out anything you wanted about me with a quick Google search."

The smell of the ocean wafts up to my nose and I glance around the kind of boat I never thought I'd step foot on.

"I'll admit I knew your favorite ice cream and what you got on your pizza when I was a kid, but other than that, I haven't checked up on you." It's mostly truth. Sure, when he came to town, Chevelle and I did a quick search to see if he was here for an acting job, but that's it.

"Well, you can rest assured you know two things about me that I don't know about you."

"You mean you still eat cookie dough ice cream, and you only eat cheese pizza?" I recite the facts that stuck with me, since those were my favorite at the time too.

He chuckles. "My palate has become more refined as far as my pizza toppings go, and these days, I'm addicted to Half Baked by Ben and Jerry's. Especially on crap days."

I press my lips together, not wanting to ask too many more questions. My mom's always told me I need to respect people's privacy more. To keep my questions to myself and wait for the person to share on their own time.

Serena returns, all smiles. "Dinner is ready inside." She steps aside like a trained model and holds her arm toward the inside of the boat.

"Oh good, I was getting a little chilly." I stand with my wineglass in hand.

"After dinner and dessert, if you two want to come back outside, we have warm blankets and a heating lamp we'll set up in the back of the boat."

We follow Serena along the side of the boat to the back, where we walk up one flight of stairs and through sliding glass doors.

"This is beautiful." I take in the tablecloth with a sprinkle of rose petals. Silverware is positioned on either side of the fine china. The napkins are twisted into an elegant shape, and there's a centerpiece of gorgeous white flowers in the middle.

Gavin comes up to the back of my chair, sliding it out for me. "Thank you, Serena," he says.

I slide between the table and the chair, and he pushes me toward the table as if he's done this his entire life.

"I have a feeling I'm not the first woman you've wooed with something like this." I should've bitten my tongue.

He positions himself in his chair, unleashing the napkin from its intricate design and laying it across his lap. When our eyes meet, he holds my gaze for a moment. "Posey, I can honestly say that I've never wanted to date a woman as much as I've wanted this date with you. I probably shouldn't tell you this, but I'm extremely nervous."

I feel the apples of my cheeks rising, unable to contain my grin. "I've never been on a date like this before." I refrain from comparing it to a fairy tale out loud, even though it's what I'm thinking. "And I'm nervous too."

He blows out a breath. "I never would've guessed."

"Really?"

Serena comes by and refills my wine while another server brings us some soup.

"You handle your nerves well." The expression on Gavin's face makes me think he's impressed by this too.

For the rest of the meal, we discuss Sunrise Bay. I fill him in on all the townie secrets, like the hidden beach spots on the bay that tourists rarely find, and give him the names and locations of all the best trails. I tell him about the bakery in Lake Starlight that's a must for donuts if you have a craving, and how Tad at Two Brothers and an Egg will memorize your order and have it in front of you in a matter of minutes. And lastly, I explain about the duo nights for the downtown businesses.

"Duo nights?" He spears some of his veggies and brings the fork to his mouth.

"The town council puts two businesses together to run an event that incorporates both businesses. It's how my brother Cade and Presley got shoved together."

"Doesn't Presley own the bookstore?" he asks.

I nod until I finish chewing my tilapia.

"And Cade's part owner of the brewery..." His forehead wrinkles.

I swallow before I laugh and sprinkle him with chewed-up fish. That would be a mood-killer for sure. "Yeah, they did a *books and beer* night. It was cute, and hey, it worked out. Now they're married and Presley's seven months pregnant."

"Another Greene on the way, huh?" His nerves seem to be fizzling out. He's becoming more of the man I see around Logan.

"As if there aren't enough of us already."

"What was that like? Growing up in Sunrise Bay?"

I widen my eyes and sip my wine because where do I even start? "I was eight when my mom moved us up here. My brother and Nikki got the brunt of the backlash. Kids my age didn't care that my mom was hooking up with my dad's cousin. But my grandparents on my dad's side and Hank's parents don't care for one another. They see Ethel as the woman who tore two brothers apart."

His jaw hangs open. "All this gossip about breakfast orders and where to go for a hike and you've been keeping a story like that all to yourself?"

I laugh and nod. "God, I'm as bad as Nikki."

"What's that like for your dad? I mean, how does he handle his cousin being married to his ex-wife?"

I feel the vault door of my heart closing. "He doesn't. My dad doesn't contact us much. He's not that close to any of us.

You know, he's got the new family and everything. But it's okay because Hank's a great stepdad."

"He's definitely protective."

We both laugh, remembering how Hank tried to intimidate Gavin. I think he was successful, not that Gavin will admit it.

"I secretly love it."

Hank being protective over me makes me believe he cares about me. That I'm just as important to him as his own kids. And since my dad doesn't really give a shit, I've always thought of Hank as more my dad than my own. If my dad met Gavin before he took me on a date, he'd probably try to hit Gavin up for some behind-the-scenes pass or for an introduction to some actor he loves. He's all about seizing an opportunity.

We finish dinner and Gavin pushes his chair away from the table. "Want to go outside?"

"Only if you keep me warm." Not my slyest line by any means.

"You kidding me? I've been dying to get you under a blanket all night." He winks and comes to pull my chair out for me.

This is the version of Gavin that I started to like at my parents' house that time. The flirtatious, slightly arrogant one.

"No roaming hands."

He raises both hands. "Promise."

Serena escorts us out to the back of the boat, where huge, thick blankets have been laid out for us. Twinkle lights are strung across the top of the boat, and little vases are filled with what look like candles but are actually lights with blue and green glass rocks.

"I might never leave, Serena," I say, sitting down.

Gavin lays the blanket over my lap before sliding in right beside me. "If this is too forward, just tell me."

My stomach feels as if bubbles are popping inside it. So far, Gavin has been a great listener, thoughtful, and a total gentleman. "Not at all."

I soak in the experience of traveling on the back of this boat that's like a scene right out of a movie. I'm so enthralled with the atmosphere that I only catch the tail end of Gavin's sentence.

"My parents love the fact I'm their son."

My gaze falls to him, and I find him staring at me. My breath hitches when our eyes lock and I see that he's opening up to me. I remain silent to allow him to take the opening if he wants it.

"They use my name to get anything from cutting in line for coffee to tickets to a show. They call my agent more than I do, and now I'm a shitty son because I'm leaving the business."

I attempt to hold in my gasp. "You are?"

"I haven't acted in two years, and I thought I'd go back after rehab, but I don't have the drive anymore. My parents gave up everything for me to be famous, and now I can't help but feel like I'm just throwing a big F-U in their faces." He sips the coffee Serena brought over a moment ago. "At first, they were on board with the rehab. I was out of control. But now, they just don't understand why I won't audition anymore."

"And why do you think you don't want to act anymore?" I feel as though I know the answer, but I don't want to speculate. I can't imagine living in the spotlight all the time and constantly being judged.

"Because I never loved it. At some point, I started to hate every minute of it."

I fight my frown.

He continues before I can say anything. "Who knows what they want for their lives at six years old? Sure, I was all in when they brought up the idea. The idea of being on television seemed fun. And at first it was. *The Carters* cast was like a second family, but then..."

I don't want to pry too much. He's clearly concerned about telling everything, but I have to admit that it makes me feel warm inside, that he's been this open with me already.

He groans. "Why are you so easy to tell all this to?"

"What do you mean?"

"I feel like I could sit here all night and tell you every little problem, all the fucked-up shit that happened, and you wouldn't judge me." He picks up his coffee, his eyes diverting from mine for the first time.

"I'd say that's a good thing, isn't it?"

He sighs and looks at me with worried eyes. "It is, but it's scary as hell. The first thing you learn in my industry is you can't trust a soul. I can't even trust my parents." He shakes his head and sets down his coffee. "This is why I wanted to keep us off this topic. Tell me something crazy about this town."

But we get interrupted because Serena tells us we're docking, and with that announcement, our magical date is over. If I were a toddler, I'd be throwing myself on the deck in a fit of kicking and screaming.

Gavin pulls out his phone and hands it to Serena. "Would you mind?"

She smiles kindly and steps back.

Gavin snuggles close and puts his arm around my shoulders. "This is just for us. Thank you for a great night," he whispers in my ear.

Tingles travel down my neck and I'm sure my cheeks are pink—and not from the wind.

Serena snaps a few pictures and hands the phone back to Gavin, then she disappears inside.

"I was going to wait until I took you home, but I want to know if you'll go out with me again?"

I nod and smile. "I'd love to."

And just like that, in one date, I find myself falling for Gavin Price. It has nothing to do with the expensive boat or the romantic setting, but rather the side of him he's trusted me with. It almost makes me feel like I can trust him too.

Chapter Seven

Gavin

I'm a coward.

The only good thing I did on our date the other night was not kiss her good night. I think she wondered why when I walked her up to her door and waited for her to get inside and lock the door. But I just didn't feel right about trying to kiss her until I have the guts to tell her what I managed to avoid all night.

But we were having such a good time that I didn't want to ruin it. I kept thinking I'd do it later and then later again, but later never came.

"So, are we just going to circle each other all fucking day?" Logan says, bouncing on the balls of his feet, circling me in the ring in his gym.

"Your wife outed me this morning," I say, still catching my breath from the last round we went before we broke.

I've been dodging talking to Logan even though he's the closest thing I have to a best friend here. Maybe ever, but I don't tell him that. It's hard to find true friends in my business, or my previous business. Logan's wife, Nikki, just took to her radio show, *Scandals of Sunrise Bay,* to tell everyone that Posey and I went on a date. Not that I wanted to keep it a secret, but the fact that the news about the mayoral race will come out any day now and I've yet to tell Posey is going to cast me as the asshole in this equation.

"Yeah, she does that." He shrugs and throws a punch that I dodge.

"I'm not sure I can tell you everything without it hitting the airwaves."

He stops and stares at me. "You don't like Posey?"

Not like Posey? I swear I'd marry the woman if it wasn't crazy. I've never met someone so genuine and pure. She honestly wanted to heal me when I told her my troubles, and I wanted to let her stitch me up. If it wasn't for this mayor thing, I think we could really be something. Over the last few days, I've contemplated withdrawing from the race. But I've always done what everyone else wanted and I want this for myself. I want to make a real difference in this world, or at least in Sunrise Bay. I can't explain why it means so much to me.

"I like her." I play it cool, then think twice. "What I mean is, I *really* like her. She's…" I shake my head, remembering her smile that lit me up inside. She's so easy to talk to.

"Damn," Logan says with a smirk.

My forehead wrinkles. "What?"

"She bit you," he says, taking off his gloves. "Come on. I'll buy you a protein shake."

We take off our gear and he grabs two protein shakes out of his fridge, then joins me so that our feet hang over the edge of the ring and our arms are on the ropes.

"Whatever you and Nikki are into is cool, but I'm not into the biting thing."

He laughs. "I meant that she's sunk her teeth into you. And I know what that's like. You're talking to a man who married someone the first night he met her and followed her up to Alaska. The Greene women have some kinda special juju."

"I do forget that sometimes." Now that they've been married for a while and have their little boy, Noah, it doesn't seem as crazy or hard to believe as when he first told me.

"Believe me, it took me a long time to win her over. Since Posey is her younger sister, I assume she has the same trust issues Nikki did because of their dad."

"She mentioned something about that." I sip my chocolate protein shake.

"I mean, I get it. We all have issues from childhood." He glances at me from the corner of his eye. He knows enough about me to know that my childhood fucked me up royally, even if I've made peace with a lot of it after I got sober.

"That's for sure. But I think I may have already destroyed it before we got our chance." I rest my forehead on the rope, my head weighing as heavy as my heart. I might've fucked up my chance at an honest relationship with a woman who appears to not care that I'm Gavin Price. Then again, I've been fooled before.

"How so?" Logan lies back and stretches his torso with his arms over his chest. "You just had your first date. Even you couldn't have screwed up that much so soon."

I roll my eyes. "Thanks for the vote of confidence." I look back at him over my shoulder. "I know you're not my therapist, but is confidentiality a thing here?" I glance around his gym.

He chuckles and sits up. "You want me to be your shrink?"

"In truth, you're the best friend I've got, but you're also married to Posey's sister and locked into the Greene family."

"I'm flattered," he says. "I think the same of you.

Remember how messed up my head was with the whole Nikki thing? Especially when she acted unfazed about the connection between us." He shakes his head.

I huff, remembering him calling me early in the morning to tell me how he got married, and she ran off. That seems so long ago now.

"I put my name in for mayor," I blurt and wait for his wrath, but Logan just looks at me for confirmation. When I nod, he falls into a fit of laughter.

"Holy shit!" He holds up his hand for me to give him a minute to catch his breath. "That's about the worst thing you could've done. You know Posey and Marla are—"

"I didn't know her mom was going to run."

He laughs again. "You need to spend more time talking to the people in this town. You're holing yourself up too much."

"Yeah, maybe." He's not wrong, but it's a habit. I'm used to not feeling free to take a walk or grab a coffee without knowing someone will snap a picture.

"People don't give a shit around here," Logan says. "You can just live your life."

"Fran and her friends had binoculars pointed at me the other day when I was running by the bay. I swear they're probably reporting my movements to the press." It's just that no one cares where I am anymore because I'm washed up, so they don't bother reporting it. At least that's what the devil on my shoulder says.

"Maybe it's different for you. I have mostly male fans since I was an MMA fighter, and you have all those girls who hung pictures of you on their walls and dreamed of marrying you when they were growing up."

I groan. At the time, I loved being a heartthrob. Talk about a huge ego boost when you're going through those awkward years. But over time, the payoff wasn't worth the price. "Anyway, back to my problem."

He pats me on the back and jumps up and out of the ring. "You're screwed. Did you know this during the date that Marla was running?"

I nod.

"Yep, kiss Posey goodbye. She is ultra-protective of her mom. I swear her mom's happiness is more important to her than her own." He grabs a sweatshirt from his gym bag and puts it on. "Nikki was convinced I was gonna cheat on her, but Posey... Posey suffers trust issues too, but, well... like I said, she's all about her mom being happy. Hate to break it to you—"

"There has to be something I can do."

He stares at me for a long time. "Obviously, the sooner you tell her, the better."

I slide through the ropes and grab my stuff before pulling on a sweatshirt. "I'll go find her now."

"I'm not saying that's gonna solve anything, but be sure to grovel. Greene girls seem to love that."

I swing my gym bag crossways over my body and hit his shoulder. "Thanks, man."

"Don't thank me yet. I still don't think you have a chance in hell."

I don't bother responding, rushing out the door, where I'm surrounded by a lot of people on the streets of Sunrise Bay.

"Gavin Price?" a woman asks with wide eyes, staring me up and down.

I nod. "Yeah. I'm sorry, I have somewhere to be." I jog down the cobblestone street, spotting Posey coming out of Fringe when I get close enough.

She stops in her tracks and looks around, a look of disgust crossing her beautiful face.

She picks up a sign and I see what's written on it.

Damn it.

"Hey, boss." Erwin comes alongside me, a bunch of signs under his arm. "I had some friends help me, so the entire downtown is filled with Vote Price signs." He smiles at me as though he's waiting for me to tell him what a good job he's doing.

My stomach plummets into my socks.

I met Erwin when he wanted to interview me for his blog, Erwin's Video Game Blog. He thought it would boost his visibility. But when he found out I don't play online games, he ended the interview, shaking his head and wondering how someone my age doesn't play games.

I don't think marketing is his forte, what with the name Erwin's Video Game Blog, but he said his mom wanted him to find a job and I needed an assistant, so here we are.

"I said to get them up next week after I get the campaign office set up."

He purses his lips. "No. You said today."

"I said next week!" I argue.

He looks at the sky, and his eyes scrunch, as if he's trying to remember. But he doesn't have to, because I know what I said.

"Let me save you some time, Erwin. I said next week. Pick them up and let's hope no one sees them."

Then a shout pulls our attention to the square. I see Posey take one of my signs, put it over her knee, and snap it in half.

"Whoa," Erwin says, his eyes bulging and his mouth hanging open. "She's scary."

"Posey!" I yell, jogging toward her.

She gets one look at me and long gone is that dreamy-eyed girl from our date. In her place is a woman who looks as if she wants to tear me limb from limb. My feet slow to walk, afraid to approach.

"What is this?" She holds up half a sign.

"I wanted to talk to you about that. The signs weren't supposed to be up yet."

"What is this?" She holds the sign up higher and her voice rises with it.

"I'm trying to explain. Can we go to your salon to talk?"

"No." Her gaze is practically burning a hole in me.

I look over her shoulder and see her entire family near a park bench, staring at us. Logan comes around the corner to join Nikki and their son.

"I did it before I found out about your mom running," I tell her.

"So you knew on our date?"

I cringe and nod.

"You son of a bitch!" Her eyes ping everywhere but on me.

"Just listen to me. It changes nothing," I say right as a strawberry milkshake hits my face.

"Are you kidding me? It changes everything!" As the milkshake drips down my face, she rushes back over to her family.

Erwin comes to my side. "You want me to get some napkins, boss?"

"I told you to call me Gavin. And yeah, that would be nice."

Erwin steps away but turns back. "Is the strawberry good? I'm usually a chocolate guy myself."

I stare at him in disbelief.

He shrugs. "I told you she was scary."

She is scary, but she's also hot as hell when she's mad. I have no idea why I'm so turned on right now, but all I want to do is take her to my house and work that scary side out of her.

Chapter Eight

Posey

"We just need to put the metal stakes in the bottoms of the signs. Rylan and Declan are going to stick them around downtown." I give the instructions to my siblings, who have agreed to help Mom with the campaign.

Mandi groans. "By the time we get Mom's out there, there will already be a sign every step."

"No, there won't. I told the boys to take the Vote Price signs down and replace them with Vote Greene."

Chevelle laughs, using all her strength to get the metal stand into the bottom of a sign. "I'll help them."

My mom comes into the room and pins me with a stare. "No, you won't. Posey, may I have a word?"

All eyes fall on me.

"Why is your sister in trouble?" I hear Declan ask Rylan.

"Looks like we're not gonna have the fun of destroying all the Vote Price signs," Rylan grumbles.

I follow my mom into the family room. She sits on the couch and I'm pretty sure I'm about to be lectured.

"Come join me." She pats the spot next to her.

I sit down and she turns to face me directly. She says my name in the same tone she's used my entire life when she wants to have a heart-to-heart but doesn't want to hurt my feelings. Everyone in this family treats me like a teacup with a hairline crack in it.

"What?" I ask.

"I really appreciate your help with this campaign. It's a bigger undertaking than I thought."

"You're welcome," I say.

"And I understand why you're upset with Gavin Price."

"He lied. I don't like liars."

A soft smile forms on her lips. "No one does, sweetie, but you also very much like Gavin, right?"

I wave my hand. "It was a good date but…"

"Well." She pats my knee. "I'm not going to have a dirty campaign. Gavin and I both want the same thing—we want to make this town a better place."

"He's lived here for a hot second."

She tilts her head, the soft smile still present. "It doesn't matter. We aren't going to take down his signs or slander his name. That's not what we're about or how I hope to win this race."

My shoulders sink and I divert my gaze from hers. "Fine."

"So you're going to play nice?"

I shrug. "Sure."

"Thank you."

"Uh-huh."

She rises from the couch and walks back into the dining room that we've transformed into campaign headquarters.

I sit for a moment, remembering my date with Gavin. I'd never felt that way with anyone before. Then again, it's not like I've been on a ton of dates. Having so many older brothers kept the boys at bay for Chevelle and me. We've always been treated as the babies.

But Gavin lied, and liars are the worst of the worst. Sure,

it was a lie by omission, but it's lying just the same. All I have to do is make sure I get my mom elected. Hopefully that will drive him out of this town. Then I can forget the magical night we shared.

Rylan comes into the living room. He and his best friend have their arms full of Vote Greene signs. "Posey, we can't hold these all on our bikes."

"I'll drive you closer into town and you can just walk." I stand and usher them out of the house. Before I leave, I go to the dining room where my mom and sisters are. "I'm taking Rylan and Declan to put up some signs. I'll be back."

"Good idea. Chevelle and I will head to the surrounding neighborhoods. Knock on some doors and stick them in people's yards that we know," Mandi says.

"And I can take them down to the fishing docks," Chevelle says.

"Let me grab my coat and go with you," my mom says.

"No. You stay. We've got this," I tell her.

We all say goodbye and leave my mom with Hank at home.

Rylan and Declan razz one another in the car, Declan making fun of Rylan about Calista, a girl from Lake Starlight who is in soccer with Rylan.

"You know you like her, just admit it," Declan says.

Rylan glances at me from the corner of his eye.

"Didn't you get her arrested?" I ask, referring to a few months ago when our older brother, Fisher, had to call Mom and Hank down to the sheriff's station.

"We weren't arrested."

"Still not a good move. Did you think about her parents? They probably think you're a delinquent now."

"You're one to talk. You're kissing Mom's enemy." Rylan sneers, and I know I hit a nerve.

Rylan isn't open about his feelings. I chalk it up to his age.

Part of me wishes he was right, and that I did get a kiss from Gavin before I knew what a liar he was, just so I would know what it's like. But it's better this way.

"You kissed Gavin Price?" Declan says from the back seat. "Does he have connections? I'd love to get Quinn Brinkley's number."

"Who's that?" I ask, turning toward the square.

"You don't know who Quinn Brinkley is?" I glance in the rearview mirror to see that he's giving me a look like what I said defies all logic.

I like Declan—he and Rylan have been friends forever—but he's one of those know-it-all kids too, just like my youngest brother.

"You wouldn't know what to do with Quinn Brinkley," Rylan says, staring out the window.

"And you'd know what to do with Calista Bailey? You can't even get up the nerve to ask her out."

Rylan says nothing.

I hold up my hand. "I want to set the record straight. I am not with Gavin Price. Once I found out he was running against Mom, I made it clear that I didn't want anything to do with him."

"By throwing a milkshake in his face. Classic." Rylan gives me a slow clap and Declan laughs.

I have a feeling these two will have a couple of milkshakes thrown in their faces during their lifetimes.

We reach downtown and I catch Fisher, his girlfriend Allie, and their twins walking into the downtown area.

"Oh shit!" I make a quick turn into one of the parking lots that surround the downtown square.

"What?" Rylan asks, looking at me as though I'm losing it.

"I'm doing Allie's hair today for a family photo session. I almost forgot."

"I hate photos. My mom makes me wear a damn Santa hat every Christmas," Declan complains.

Maybe this is why he and Rylan are best friends. Rylan is the quiet type and Declan can't stop talking.

"You guys have this handled?" I ask Rylan as I park.

"Yeah, we'll just walk home after." Rylan exits my car.

My chest squeezes. Rylan seems so downtrodden. I make a mental note to talk to him later or send over one of my male siblings. Anyone but Xavier. I'm not sure I know who he is these days, and I can't chance him giving Rylan bad advice.

"Thanks, guys!" I wave as I rush off.

The bell rings when I enter Fringe.

Malia raised eyebrows says she's surprised to see me.

"Yeah, I forgot I'm doing Allie's hair." I quickly put on my apron.

I'm tying up the back as the happy family comes in. Everyone in the waiting room ohhs and ahhs over the twins. Fisher watches them like a hawk while Allie kisses his cheek and heads over to me.

She plops down in the chair. "I've been waiting for this forever." She sighs.

The woman needs a masseuse, not a hairstylist. Raising twins has got to suck every ounce of energy from you.

I put my hands on her shoulders and squeeze. "Just relax and enjoy."

Fisher grunts as another woman enters the salon and tries to put her hand in the stroller. "I'm out. I'll be back to pick you up, Allie."

Without another word, he pushes the double stroller out of the small waiting room and back out to the streets of Sunrise Bay.

"He's so protective of them." Allie looks at me through the mirror.

I color and cut Allie's hair, giving her a fresh look. We chat about this and that, but she's respectful enough not to ask me any questions about Gavin Price or the election. Instead, we discuss the trials of raising babies with an over-protective partner like Fisher, which we chalk up to the fact that he's the sheriff.

Fisher returns as I'm finishing with Allie, and he heads to my office to change into his clothes for the photo shoot. It says a lot that Allie got him to agree to this.

Allie disappears after Fisher while everyone in the waiting room coos over the babies. I'm annoyed when sex sounds leak out of my office. Especially the pounding on the wall. The worst part isn't that they're having sex in my office, it's that I want to be the one having sex in my office. It's been over a year since I've slept with anyone, and he was a medi-ocre partner at best.

Finally they emerge, Allie's cheeks red and Fisher looking like the prize stud at a horse auction.

"Did you know that Gavin Price moved in next door?" Fisher asks, thumbing in the direction of the shop next door.

Irritation fires up like a struck match inside me. I toss the brush in my hand on the counter. "What?"

"He's setting up his campaign headquarters there, I think. There's a bunch of Vote Price signs stacked along the wall."

I hope for Gavin's sake that Fisher is mistaken.

I stomp out of the salon, hearing Fisher laugh behind me while Allie reprimands him for telling me.

I get to where our two shops meet and lean forward to get a glimpse into the storefront beside my salon. Sure enough, there he is in a button-down shirt with the sleeves rolled up and a pair of slacks. Gavin's arranging papers on one of the desks and that guy is with him again. The one who was sticking signs around downtown.

My mom's words ring in my head.

"Play nice, Posey," I say to myself.

I straighten my back and open his office door. There's no bell, so I overhear the two of them talking about going door-to-door until the assistant spots me from the corner of his eye. He hits Gavin, then Gavin's gorgeous blue eyes are on me.

My knees grow weak under the force of his stare. I can't deny the feelings he evokes inside me. There's no explaining it.

"This is your new headquarters?" I look around.

"Yeah, it's not nearly up to snuff yet though." Gavin walks toward me. "Erwin, go get some coffee," he says, his eyes never leaving mine. Then my name comes out of his lips as if I'm his savior and his tormentor all in one.

I'm familiar with the feeling.

"I just wanted to..." My apology gets stuck in my throat.

"It's all on me. I wanted to tell you. Erwin wasn't supposed to put up those signs when he did. You were so excited for your mom and our date was going so well... I didn't want to mess it up."

How very selfish of him, but I'm going to play nice because my mom asked me to.

"It's fine, Gavin." I look at the right side of his head where there's a long strand out of place. I must've somehow missed it when I cut his hair last week. I step forward and his eyes fall to my lips. We're millimeters apart and the scent of his cologne stirs my arousal. I motion to the piece of hair. "I missed this piece last week."

His hand goes to it and my breath hitches, desperate for him to touch me. "I parted it differently. I was in a rush."

"Let me fix it," I say softly, my eyes locked with his.

"Okay."

A knock on the window pulls us away from one another. We both turn to find Erwin there.

"What kind of coffee do you like?" he shouts through the glass.

Gavin groans and waves him in. "Forget the coffee, just keep straightening everything up. I'll be right back."

Gavin follows me into Fringe. All movement and gossip halts at our entry. But I ignore it.

I seat him in the chair, put the cape over him, then take him to the shampoo bowl. Probably because I want to torture myself while I watch his facial expressions that show just how much he loves it when my fingers weave through his strands and rub his scalp. As he did the time before, his eyes close and he makes the cutest little sounds of enjoyment.

Once he's in the chair, all eyes remain on us. I comb out his hair, positioning his part.

"Your hair grows fast," I say, deciding to clean up the entire hairstyle.

"Yeah, I usually have to go every two and a half weeks."

I clip the little ends to freshen up his cut. My phone rings and I set everything down to answer. Usually I would never, but this is Gavin, after all. He can wait. Mandi tells me that Fisher and Allie just got engaged down by the bay. I'm happy for them, but a touch of melancholy festers inside me. I'm starting to doubt that I'll ever get what they have.

I get back to cutting Gavin's hair and I don't make small talk, too inside my head to bother.

But Gavin seems to want to talk. "Does this mean you forgive me then?"

And all that anger at his lie surfaces again. The reminder that he's not who I thought he was makes my whole body tense. My fingers slip and the scissors nick his ear.

"Ouch!" he yells and stands, covering his ear.

When he pulls his hand away, blood coats his palm. He shakes his head, giving me a look like I'm batshit crazy.

"Gavin, I'm sorry! My scissors just slipped. That's never happened before."

Allie, Fisher, and the twins are returning at that moment and Allie rushes to Gavin's side.

"Are you okay?" she asks. "I'm a nurse."

He shakes his head. "You Greenes are nuts." He removes his hand, and blood drips from his ear to the floor.

"You'll be okay," Allie says.

Gavin rushes away from her as though he just found out she's a serial killer the police have been searching for. "I'll take someone else's opinion, thank you."

Gavin goes into his office next door as Fisher catches up with Allie. They both set their eyes on me.

"What? The scissors slipped."

Fisher points at me. "If I have to arrest you tonight, I'm warning you right now, you're rotting in jail until tomorrow. I better not be disturbed tonight."

"Oh, that's right! Congratulations, guys. Let me see!" I walk over to congratulate them and see the ring.

They look at me as if I'm delusional and maybe I am, but honestly, the scissors slipped. At least that's the story I'm sticking with.

Chapter Nine

Posey

Later that day, I come downstairs at home to find Mandi baking in the kitchen while Nikki's radio show is on.

"Can you please turn it off?" I say, grabbing an orange juice and sitting on the other side of the breakfast bar.

Mandi doesn't answer, just gives me a look.

"Why are you baking?" I ask.

She blows one of her red strands out of her eyes. "Francois said he could bake better than me, so I'm challenging him."

"Can we please just call him Frank?" I grumble.

Mandi's chef at the inn is so arrogant, he insists everyone call him Francois. But really his name is Frank, and he's from Alaska. He's just a brilliant chef who never trained professionally.

"Shh... his radar will go off knowing there's a disturbance in the force and I'll have to listen to him complain about it for a solid week."

I sip my orange juice while I listen to Nikki's retelling of the scene I was a part of yesterday.

"And then she cut his ear. Rumor has it he went screaming home like a little boy," Nikki says.

Mandi eyes me over the cup of flour she's leveling.

"I'd be screaming too. It's kind of scary, you know?" Chip, her sidekick, chimes in.

"Oh, Posey's not scary. She's just spiteful." Nikki laughs. "I think it's because she likes him and he hurt her. Why are men so stupid sometimes?"

"Do you really want me to answer that?" Chip asks.

"No, Chip, I mean, when was your last date? I think we should do a new segment following you on a dating app." Nikki does have some great ideas. "We can see who you match with and when you go on dates, you can report back to us in the morning."

"Never gonna happen."

"You're a mean man, Chip. Anyway, back to my sister," Nikki says.

"You owe me. You said double or nothing after you were wrong about Fisher." Chip has a point.

Mandi and I look at each other and laugh.

"First of all, they're engaged now. So I was a few months off." I can picture Nikki rolling her eyes.

Mandi rations out each ingredient and I finish my orange juice, unsure why I'm enduring this torture.

"That's why it's a bet, Nikki. You can't say, 'Well, the horse won three races after I bet on him to win, so I get the money.' And I guarantee you right now, Posey and Gavin are never going to get together."

Nikki scoffs. "This is why you need to go on a dating app. You know nothing about women."

"She threw a milkshake in his face and now she's causing him bodily injury. What could I possibly be missing?"

"Sometimes I think you live in the Dark Ages," Nikki says. "To everyone else out there, keep your eye on these two. We're in for a fun mayoral campaign because one thing I know for sure is that my sister plays dirty. You should've seen her play Monopoly when we were kids—ruthless."

Mandi laughs so hard she spills the vanilla extract in her batter.

"Too much vanilla flavoring never hurt anyone," I say, dipping my finger in. I lick the batter off, but I can barely swallow it, it's so thick. Hopefully the extra vanilla helps.

"Very true." She pours in a little more.

"Posey Ida Greene!" my mom yells from behind me, and I startle. I didn't even hear her come in.

"Pig," Mandi says, laughing.

I pick up a pinch of flour and toss it at her face.

Yes, not only was I tormented to have a grandma middle name like Ida, but my initials spell pig. I'll let you imagine what that was like growing up.

"Hey, I need my eyes to see." Mandi wipes the flour from her face, but there's still residue in the crease of her nose. "You know why she's here."

My mom walks into the kitchen. I'm surprised it's taken her this long to hear the news actually. And I'm sure I have Nikki and her damn show to thank for it.

Mandi turns down the volume since Nikki and Chip are moving on to other happenings that aren't as juicy as me cutting Gavin's ear. People act like I turned him into Van Gogh. Jeez.

"Hi, Mom," Mandi says with a big smile and wave.

Mom looks at Mandi with confusion because Mandi's not one to bake. Usually everything is left to Frank at the inn.

Shaking her head, Mom turns her attention to me. Her hands rest on her hips. "Well?"

"What?" I feign ignorance.

"You cut his ear? I thought we had a conversation about this."

I stand from the breakfast stool, mostly to get away from her scathing look. "It was an accident. I wouldn't cut someone on purpose. It could ruin my business."

Not really. Maybe if it was Fran. She might hurt my business with all her reporting on Sunrise Bay social media page.

"I'm the acting mayor right now. I'm not sure how clear I need to make this. You don't have to like him, but you do have to be cordial. There will be a lot of events we're both going to be at, and if you can't control yourself around him, then I'll have to find myself a new campaign manager."

"Good luck with that," Mandi says under her breath.

"Excuse me?" Mom asks.

Mandi's head flies up. "Did I say that out loud?"

"Yes, you did." I pat her on the back. But I want to help my mom achieve her goal, to see her smile on that platform when she wins and know I had something to do with her happiness. "I'll go apologize... again."

"Thank you," my mom says with a nod and a small smile, then she turns her attention to my sister. "What are you baking, Mandi?"

"Muffins? I think."

Mom looks at the chocolate chip batter in a molding pan. "Good luck." She swipes her finger through the batter and tastes it. "That's a lot of vanilla."

"Good, right?" Mandi smiles and waits for my mom's approval.

She forces a smile. "Really good, Mandi."

"Can I have a few to take to Gavin with my apology?" I ask Mandi in an innocent voice.

Mom's eyes narrow, but she's not going to say anything

and risk hurting Mandi's feelings. If the muffins end up tasting like the batter, then eating them will be more punishment than apology.

"Sure." Mandi places the trays in the oven.

"Don't worry, Mom, I'll make it all good again." I put my arm around her shoulders, and she eyes me with mistrust. As they say, mother knows best, and my mom's got my number.

WITH MY MUFFINS in a cute red tin leftover from the Christmas cookie exchange we did last year at Fringe, I open the door to Gavin's campaign headquarters.

He's done a lot of work in only a day. A water cooler and coffee station sit by the window. Desks are cleaned off, each with a phone, a penholder, and some office supplies.

"Hey, Erwin," I say.

"Miss Greene." He nods.

"Erwin, I've known you since kindergarten. Do not call me Miss Greene," I say with a roll of my eyes.

"Boss man would like me to refer to people with Mr. and Mrs. while I'm working for him."

"Well, that's stupid," I say, and the huff from the back of the room steals my attention.

Gavin says my name like a warning to leave. He rises from the biggest desk in the back. Of course, he has the biggest desk.

Overcompensate much?

I hold up the tin with what I hope seems to be a genuine smile. "I just wanted to apologize yet again for my misstep."

He walks down the aisle of desks. "You bake?"

Hmm... I'm not sure how to answer that, since I didn't

bake these and I rarely bake, but I have baked in the past, so I answer, "Yes, I bake on occasion." Not a lie.

I pass the tin to him. He lifts the lid, looks inside, then shuts it before sliding it across the desk to me. "Thanks for the thought, but I'd rather not end up in the hospital with food poisoning."

"They're not going to make you sick," I argue.

He raises his eyebrows and stares at me, crossing his arms. His forearms are corded with muscles. Ugh, why do I care?

"Why would I trust you after you threw a milkshake at me and nearly cut my ear off?"

I lean to the side to look at his ear. There's a bandage covering it. "Looks intact to me."

"You cut my ear," he says, shaking his head.

"And I'm apologizing by giving you these muffins." God, this guy tries my patience. I slide the tin back across the desk.

"Like I said, no thanks." He slides the tin back.

I roll my eyes.

"I'll have a muffin," Erwin says.

We both turn our attention to him, and he slithers back toward his desk.

"Fine." I open the tin. "I'll eat one, then you'll know they aren't poisoned." Grabbing a muffin, I hold it up to my mouth, saying a quick and silent prayer.

He leans back and waits for me to take a bite.

"You know how childish this is, right?" I say, working up the nerve to eat this muffin.

"I don't think it's childish. I think I'm making sure I don't die today."

His smirk aggravates me, and I'm left wondering why I ever thought his boyish good looks were attractive. Who am

I kidding? This attitude of his is turning me on more than when he was a perfect gentleman on our date.

I lean forward, taking a big bite of the muffin, exaggerating my chewing while crumbs fall down my shirt onto the desk below. God, it's dry and cakey. I continue to chew and chew, the pastry forming a solid ball of dry goop in my mouth. I'm barely able to swallow it, but I manage, coughing after.

"See?" I say with a hoarse voice. "I ate it and I'm still here."

He lifts his wrist where his expensive silver watch rests. "We'll give it ten minutes or so, no?"

Again, I roll my eyes, glancing at the water cooler. It looks so refreshing right now.

"I'll take a muffin. I trust Posey." Erwin rolls his chair over, staring into the tin.

"Erwin, please make your phone calls," Gavin tells him, denying him the muffin. Which is good. I'd rather just get out of here and afterward they can talk about how horrible they taste.

"Well..." I clear my throat. "I have to get to work now." I hold out my arms. "See? I'm alive."

"You won't mind if I wait to make sure the ambulance doesn't show up anytime soon."

"Suit yourself." I turn to walk out of his office.

He says my name, and this time it isn't with the same disdain it held a few minutes ago. I slowly turn.

"Make sure you bring enough water for the 10K race. I heard a rumor that our drink stations are right across from one another on the race route."

"What?" I didn't know anything about this.

"Did your mom already fire you? What with you giving her a bad reputation and all?"

I smack on a smile, not allowing him to get to me. "Don't play games you can't win, Gavin."

Erwin squeaks, and his eyes flit from me to Gavin and back.

"Oh, I'm gonna win, Posey. I tend to get what I want."

A scream lodges in my throat at his arrogance. Where's the sweet man from the date? I knew he was too good to be true.

"Not if I can help it."

"Game on. See you at the race then." He picks up the tin and tosses it on Erwin's desk. "Next time your mom makes you apologize to me, try and remember that I'm a sugar cookie kinda guy." He winks.

I hate the fact that my stomach flips. I narrow my eyes, a million snappy remarks on the tip of my tongue, but I have to honor my mom's wishes. "See you at the race, Gavin. Can't wait."

He chuckles lightly.

I walk out of his campaign headquarters, into Fringe, right into my office, where I finally release my scream.

Chapter Ten

Gavin

Sunday morning, I'm setting up my refreshment table at the race. Erwin is supposed to be bringing down all the water. I put a Vote Price sign up on the table, along with a few around the grass. Not wanting to ask any of the Greenes to help me since Marla's competing, I recruited a few Bailey kids to help pass out pins and stickers.

I worried at first that the Sunrise Bay residents would only see me as an outsider, but so far, people have been pretty responsive to me.

Erwin walks down the hill to meet me at the path along the bay, which is the halfway mark for the runners. I stare at how much water he has. One case. As in twenty-four bottles.

"Erwin?" I raise an eyebrow.

"Yeah, boss?"

"We have more water in the vehicle, right? Like, all the water I had delivered?"

He squints as though he's trying to recollect, but struggling. A look I've become familiar with since he started working for me. "You want *all* that water?"

"There will be more than twenty-four racers," I say.

"Sure, but the Greenes will be handing out water as well."

"Just go get the rest of the water."

He takes the wagon he borrowed from his sister and trudges back up the hill. Meanwhile, I catch sight of Posey walking toward me. Two teenage boys follow her with a wagon similar to Erwin's. She looks mouthwatering in yoga pants and a sweatshirt that's stretched across her delicious tits. The night of our date, the tease of her cleavage made me wonder what her nipples look like. Are they silver dollars or small Hershey's Kisses?

"Oh hey, Gavin," she says, waving to me from across the path.

I snap out of my daze of imagining her naked. If I don't get these feelings out of my head, I'm screwed.

"Posey." I nod. One boy opens up the table they've brought, and Rylan, who I recognize as her little brother, puts up their signs. "Good thing you brought help."

She raises her eyebrows. "I could've done it myself."

I hold up both hands and turn toward the bay, away from her. Maybe it's just better if we don't converse.

"Gavin!" Jack Thorne spots me and runs down the hill, tripping and rolling, but the kid recovers as if he meant to do it all along.

Maverick runs down and swoops him up. If gaming doesn't get that kid famous, he might have a future as a stuntman. Behind Maverick is a dark-haired girl who keeps looking around as though she's waiting to spot someone as she walks slowly down the hill.

"Looks like I'm not the only one who brought help?" Posey's snarky retort has me looking back at her.

"Well, I don't have a huge family."

"So you pick Griffin and Phoenix Thornes' kids. Interesting." She inhales a deep breath and cocks her hip. "Just so you know, the Baileys don't have the pull here that they do in Lake Starlight. Right, Rylan?"

Posey smacks him in the stomach with her hand, but he doesn't flinch. Because his eyes are fixed on the teenage girl walking down the hill.

"Hey, we brought our cousin," Maverick says when he reaches me and puts Jack down. "That's okay, right?"

"The more help, the better," I say, more interested in what's happening between Rylan and their cousin. "What's her name?"

"Calista. She's our Uncle Rome's oldest. Is this all the water you have? Because it's not gonna be enough." Maverick looks from the water back to me.

"My assistant is grabbing some more. Thanks for bringing your cousin. Seems like she's gonna do a great job of distracting one of Posey's helpers." I smile across the way.

Posey hammers me with a pissed-off expression. Erwin was right, she has a feisty side that's a little scary.

"Rylan." She snaps her fingers in front of his face.

"You might as well forget it; he's done for the day. Trust me." Rylan's friend continues to pour water from the bottles into cups on the table. I'm told that's so they can down some water and toss the paper cup aside while they're running, to be picked up later.

Another glare from Posey only keeps my smile in place. I get some sick sense of pleasure at throwing her off-kilter.

Calista finally comes all the way down the hill. Her gaze keeps going to Rylan, making me feel as though I'm in some reenactment of a teenage drama I once starred in.

"Okay, I'm going to stay here and pass out the paper cups, but I need one of you to go with Erwin to the finish line and pass out actual water bottles for when they finish the race. When you give them one, say vote Price."

As I finish talking, a golf cart pulls up. Inside are Ethel Greene and Dori Bailey, who I've met a few times.

"Isn't this fun?" Dori steps out and comes to my side before encompassing Calista in a big hug, then she moves on to Jack and Maverick.

Ethel walks over to Posey, and I hear her explain how my team will be handing out water at the finish line. Posey looks at me over Ethel's shoulder. The two of them whisper, and suddenly, Rylan is on the back of the golf cart with a few cases of water and Ethel in the driver's seat.

"Hey, Gavin, good luck today," Ethel says, waving at me in what feels like a condescending way.

I nod. "Thank you, Mrs. Greene."

"I'm going to take Calista then." Dori swings her arm around the young girl, whose cheeks are now red like a stoplight.

"Okay, Erwin will meet you over there with the water," I say, fine with Calista going. Hopefully the two kids will equal each other out.

Calista sits in the back of the golf cart next to Rylan, and the two of them are clearly trying to stay as far apart from one another as possible.

Meanwhile, Maverick fills the water cups until the entire table is full. Declan does the same for Posey, and I figure this is a fair fight. Until Hank and Marla come down the hill with pieces of plywood in their arms.

"Great. Mom's here," Posey says too loudly.

They put the plywood over their water cups so they can have three stacks of filled water cups.

"Shit, this isn't their first time doing this," Maverick says, standing next to me and watching them accomplish a move that will probably seal their win. It might seem silly to compete over water, but I've always been competitive, and it's clear to me that Posey has that same competitive spirit.

Once they're finished, Posey comes over to me. "So, we

never did make a wager, or are you too scared now that you see our setup?"

I widen my stance and put my hands in my pockets, leaning forward. "You don't scare me, Greene."

"Good, then whoever gives out the most water by the end of the race is the winner. And you have to be honest with your count. No cheating."

"And what do you want if you win?" I ask, already knowing exactly what I'm going to ask for.

She pretends to think about it.

"It has to be within reason. I'm not pulling myself out of the election, nor am I moving my campaign headquarters." I cross my arms.

Her lips purse and suddenly I really wish I would've snagged one kiss from those rosy lips before all the shit went down between us.

"I'll go first," I say. "If I win, you cut my hair for free every two weeks for the next year."

She scoffs. "Two weeks? You can at least go three weeks."

I shake my head. "Three weeks and I'm shaggy. I am trying to win an election." I wink and her eyes narrow.

Her eyes bore into mine. "Fine. But if I win, I get to cut your hair however I want. Even shave it all off if I see fit."

Damn. She's evil. I glance back at our water, then at her water tower.

"I like that look on you," she says, twirling her pointer finger in my face.

"What look?"

"Fear. Like turkey around Thanksgiving."

I huff and stick out my hand. "Deal."

Her small, soft hand glides into mine and all I want to do is tug her into my arms, hug her small body, and kiss her forehead.

"Gavin, so nice of you to come out and support our local runners." Marla's appearance pulls me out of the moment, and Posey is quick to drop my hand. But I catch Marla noticing.

"Yes, you as well, Mrs. Greene."

Marla tilts her head. "Oh, Marla, please."

"Okay, Marla." I put out my hand. "Nice to see you again."

Her handshake is much firmer than her daughter's.

The announcement comes that the race is about to start, so we end our conversation and I go back to my table.

"Okay, Maverick and Jack, you need to keep count of every cup of water you give out." I lean in as though we're in a football huddle and we can't let the opposing team hear us. "Jack, use those brown puppy-dog eyes to get the runners to come to you. Maverick, keep refilling and any girls around your age, use flirting to your advantage."

They both nod, and I pray that Erwin and Calista do great at the finish line.

IT TAKES over twenty minutes before a runner reaches us. Posey rushes to him, saying hello using his actual name.

"Vote Greene, Mato," she says, handing him a cup of water. She shrugs after he passes. "He's a police officer with my brother."

Two more people come, and we each pass a water to one. Which means she's still up by one.

My phone vibrates in my pocket, and I pull it out to see a message from her. It's a picture of a guy who has a multicolored mohawk. I pocket my phone and narrow my eyes at her.

More runners come, and Jack is able to swindle some older women over to our side. They all say what a cutie he is, and he smiles, handing them water.

I raise my eyebrows at Posey, and she just rolls her eyes.

I take out my phone and send her a text message.

> Might as well mark it on your calendar now. Every two weeks.

The three dots appear, and I look up to see Marla and Hank handing out water. Declan is sitting back in a chair, messing around on his phone.

> Aren't you afraid the scissors might slip again??

She attaches a GIF of Edward Scissorhands.

A rush of runners are coming, so I slide my phone into my pocket and grab some cups to pass out. There are so many people that the runners don't show preference, but just take whatever cup they can. Maverick refills another row and I see one piece of the Greene's plywood hit the ground because they're done with the top level.

Great, I might be campaigning with a mohawk.

The middle pack of runners don't give us much breathing time, or time to text one another, which is unfortunate because all I keep thinking about is what she'll send me next.

We get to the point that some of the runners are taking their own waters off the tables. A man slows and tells Jack to pour a cup over his head, bending over so the little guy can do so. We're fortunate that a few others copy the motion. Jack thinks it's the best thing ever, and it's helping us get rid of water, so it's a win as far as I'm concerned.

"Those don't count!" Posey points and screams over the runners' heads.

"We never said the water had to be consumed," I say.

She inhales deeply and Marla turns to her, probably asking her what is going on. I wonder if Posey will tell her about the bet.

The race keeps us busy for another half hour. I had no idea how big this run was until right now. But as quickly as the big group came through, it slows to one runner here, one runner there.

How's it going over there?

I glance up to see her relaxing in the chair Declan was in. He's gone and I assume he's up with Rylan at the finish line. They're on their last row of cups. We checked in on our counts about a half hour ago and were neck and neck so we both poured out an equal remainder of cups. Whoever gets rid of all of those first will be the winner. I only have to get rid of these cups on the table before her, and I should be good.

You know how much I spend on haircuts?
It'll be nice to get them for free.

She doesn't respond, and a small group comes through and mostly goes to Posey's side. From the bits of conversation I hear, they must know one another. Then Fran and her gang come down the path.

I smile. I'm pretty sure they'll come to me.

"Fran!" I exclaim, clapping. "Way to go, ladies."

All their cheeks are already pink, so I have no idea if I made them blush.

"Gavin," they say in unison.

"Maverick, come out from behind the table."

He picks up a few cups of water and we hold them out.

"Fran!" Posey yells. "Sunrise Bay born and bred." She points at herself.

I shake my head at her.

"You can call me Blake Michaels." I hate it when people use my character name from *High Society*, but I will not be able to pull off some absurd haircut while I'm campaigning, and I know Posey has the guts to give me one.

"Sorry, Posey," Fran says. "Blake," she coos, and I ignore the nausea.

They stop instead of walking past, which sucks because the other runners coming up are now at the Greene table since mine is blocked. The good news is that the women all drink more than one cup. By the time they leave, I'm out of water.

I pull out my phone

Look up.

Posey glances from her phone over to us, and that's when I realize that their table is empty too. This sucks. We never decided anything about a tie.

I'm trying to think what we can agree on with a tie. Until her smirk forms a frown, and she questions Hank and Marla. They each shrug. Hank's already packing up.

The two grandmas return with the golf cart, Erwin on the back.

I walk over to Posey. "Is that frown an indication that you'll have to put me in your planner?"

She takes a deep breath. "I'm going to kill Declan, but yes, apparently we have water left at the finish line and you're out."

I tsk and chuckle. "Sorry you lost."

"Don't be condescending."

"I'm not. I am sorry, but I'm happier that I won." I smirk and walk backward. She watches me go and slowly her hands move toward a cup of water she was drinking earlier. She wrote her name on it after I insisted so that it wouldn't get mixed up in the count. She picks it up and walks toward me. "What are you doing?"

"Posey!" Marla yells.

She's already mid throw and I run into a body, moving out of the way right before the water douses Erwin. He stares at Posey in disbelief and a low whine erupts out of him.

"Oh my god, I'm sorry," Posey says.

Erwin shakes his head in disbelief and stomps away. "Scary. Scary. Scary."

Posey glares at me and all I can do is smile. Because if I was honest about what I really want to do to her right now, people would think I'm crazy. What can I say? I've always liked a woman who puts her feelings out there for all to see.

Chapter Eleven

Posey

I swear the entire town of Sunrise Bay has congregated in the high school auditorium.

I'm with my mom in my old English classroom while she has her makeup touched up by Nikki. I have no idea where Gavin is, but I can feel him in this building, which sounds crazy.

It's been just over a week since the race, and I haven't talked to Gavin, but I have had to endure seeing him dressing all sexy in slacks and button-downs. Sometimes he mixes it up with V-neck sweaters and ties. In the evenings when I'm closing down my shop, I purposely walk by his building and see him with his shirtsleeves rolled up his forearms and his head buried in something. I'm woman enough to admit that his arm porn is on point.

From what I've witnessed, I'm pretty sure Gavin's taking this mayor thing seriously and not just doing it to pass time.

"Posey, ask me some practice questions," my mom says, her eyelids shut while Nikki puts on eyeshadow.

"How do you plan to bring technology into the schools?" I ask a question I know for certain will be asked by the moderator, George Lehmann. Not sure how he got selected since he probably doesn't know what technology is available for the youth these days. They probably didn't even have calculators when he attended Sunrise Bay Elementary.

My mom answers the question, but my mind drifts back to Gavin and the flirtatious way he eggs on the competitiveness between us. Almost like he's playing games with me.

"Was that good?" Mom asks.

"Perfect," Nikki answers. "Right, Posey?"

I sit up straight, needing to focus on what's ahead. "Yes. You're ready. Do you need anything?"

My mom inhales a nervous breath.

Hank clears his throat from across the room and stands from one of the desks. "Do you girls mind leaving your mom and me alone for a moment?"

"Sure." Nikki collects her things and nods to me to follow her. I'm forever the little sister. "No messing up the makeup and hair I just did, Hank."

He does the scout's honor salute as we step into the hall.

Right before I shut the door, I hear Hank tell Mom, "You've got this, baby. You're meant to run this town."

The best thing that happened to Mom was Hank Greene. He took her heart from an empty, bottomless pit to overflowing with love. The minute he came to pick her up on a date, I knew it, which is probably why I gave him a little bit of a hard time. I didn't want someone to hurt her again like my dad had and I saw on her face as she got ready that night how important Hank was to her.

"Relationship goals, right?" Nikki whispers, and I nod.

We walk down the hallway toward the auditorium, and I spot Logan at the end of the hall with Noah in his arms. I watch as he pulls Nikki to him and kisses her lips, then her temple as she takes Noah from him.

She's talking about relationship goals when she had an MMA fighter follow her up here and beg her to stay married to him. Sometimes I wonder if I'll ever find someone who loves me like that.

"Boo," someone whispers right beside my ear.

I yelp and turn to find Gavin standing there.

"Jesus." My hand covers my heart. "Are you trying to scare me to death? Actually, maybe I'd thank you. It would be nice not to have to hear you drone on and on tonight."

He smiles instead of looking annoyed. It's like he's getting off on our arguing. "Funny. I'd listen to you talk about stocks and bonds and never be bored."

I point at him. "Don't you dare play mind games with me, Price."

He chuckles, his hands sliding into his slacks as he rocks back on his heels. I notice for the first time what he's wearing. A suit.

A suit that fits him perfectly.

A suit that's perfectly tailored to his leanly muscled body.

All I want to do is slowly undress him, button by button, then slide down his zipper and watch his slacks fall to the floor. My hand would run over his thick length that would tent what I assume are black boxer briefs.

I blink because his face is right in front of mine. "Posey?" he says in a low voice. "Stop imagining me naked."

I blink and come back to myself, scoffing. "In your dreams."

"You're right."

I shake my head and scowl, not understanding. "What?"

"In my dreams, you *would* be picturing me naked and..." His gaze travels up and down the hallway before he leans in and lowers his voice. "Imagining me fucking you."

My body betrays me. An electric current travels from

head to toe, my stomach flutters, and an unbearable ache starts between my legs. Damn him to hell.

Lucky for me, Mom and Hank come out of the classroom and start down the hall. She looks a little flushed, but her makeup and hair are still on point.

"Gavin." Mom walks over with her hand extended.

He winks before turning away from me. Gavin shakes my mom's hand, then Hank's, who doesn't seem all that thrilled, but he's never rude.

"Good luck tonight, Gavin," my mom says, sounding genuine. How does she remain so gracious?

"You as well. You definitely have the advantage. I feel like I'm presenting at the Emmys all over again."

My mom tilts her head. "Wouldn't those be your colleagues and friends?"

Gavin frowns momentarily but recovers. "You'd think, but no."

"Well, Sunrise Bay is always welcoming to new residents. They'll be nice. Don't worry." Mom runs her hand down the length of his arm in a motherly caress.

I look at her with a puzzled expression, because what the hell?

"Thanks. I don't think you should be giving me a pep talk." Gavin chuckles.

"The mom inside will never leave her." Hank takes her hand. "We'll see you two in there."

They walk away and my mom rests her head on Hank's shoulder. At the doors, he whispers something in her ear.

"They're pretty great," Gavin says.

I nod. It might be the only thing we've agreed on lately. "I better go."

"No good-luck kiss?" Gavin asks after I step away.

"No, but I can offer you a good luck kick in the nuts."

With an evil cackle, I turn on my heel and head toward the auditorium to grab my seat.

I want a front row view of the shit show.

I'M SITTING in the front row when Ethel comes along one side of me and Dori on the other. They sandwich me in, and I can't help but feel like this is some kind of trap. These two are never not up to something.

"Thank goodness we're not late," Dori whispers, sounding out of breath.

"We had to lose Sheriff Miller. I let Dori drive."

I whip my head in her direction. "Grandma!"

She shrugs. "What? We only have a few years left. We need some excitement in our lives." She pats my knee. "Oh…"

I follow her gaze to the stage where Gavin sits relaxed with one leg propped up on his knee and his arm out behind the empty chair beside him, talking to George Lehmann.

"He's a looker. No wonder he was such a star." Dori elbows me and I'm positive there will be a bruise there tomorrow morning.

The rest of my family takes their seats, each of them snickering at the position I'm in between my grandma and Dori.

"I guess Posey's their next victim," Fisher whispers to Allie behind me.

"Good luck to her," Jed chimes in.

I give them a scathing look over my shoulder.

George Lehman clears his throat then taps the mic, which makes a loud screeching sound ring throughout the auditorium.

"Want to go make out under the bleachers?" Cade whispers, not quietly enough, to Presley.

"Sure, babe, I'm seven months pregnant. I'd love to fold myself under metal stands and make out with you."

I'm pretty sure she's being sarcastic, but George interrupts the secondary conversations from my family.

"Okay, I'm going to introduce everyone to our two candidates running for Sunrise Bay mayor. First off, we have our current acting mayor, Marla Greene. Who doesn't know Marla? From the fact that she married her ex-husband's cousin to the fact that she makes the best salad dressings in the state. She grew up here. This was her high school. There isn't anyone or anything Marla doesn't know about Sunrise Bay. Let's give her a hand."

The crowd claps—I whistle, of course—while my mom walks over to her podium on the right side.

"Second, many of you know him, or think you do, from his successful television shows, a few B movies and tabloid fodder. Gavin Price recently moved to Sunrise Bay after visiting us off and on for a couple years. Although we don't know much about him, the women of this town sure seem to like to drool over his daily runs in the park. Let's give him a warm Sunrise Bay welcome."

Gavin's smile loses its sparkle for a moment due to the introduction, but when a whole section of moms cheer and whistle for him, he raises his hand in a wave with a nod of thanks, making his way to his podium.

I roll my eyes at the group cheering him on. I went to high school with some of them. No surprise they're all in their twenties or early thirties—the generation that was head over heels in love with Blake Michaels, aka Gavin Price.

"Those women should be ashamed," Dori whispers. "Everyone knows he only has eyes for you."

My head whips in her direction. "We don't even like each other."

"You sure about that?" Dori asks.

"Yes," I answer, knowing I'm not.

George says a few things about the rules for the night, then gets right into it. "First question, how do you plan on getting the schools more up to speed as far as technology goes? Marla, you can take this one first."

George motions to my mom, who smiles at the crowd. "When I was growing up, we didn't have tablets or computers. We had a pencil and paper. And although I feel my generation turned out just fine, I understand that we can't let our children fall behind on available technology. So I propose that we have fundraisers. There are many programs that I was a part of when my kids were younger, like box tops and can tabs. The kids are then part of it, which makes receiving the new technology more rewarding for them."

"Thanks, Marla. Gavin, your turn," George says.

"As much as I think the kids should be part of earning the reward of a computer or tablet, I don't think technology is a privilege, but a must. If we don't get them into their hands soon, there's no doubt our kids will fall behind other kids their age. This is a necessity. I know when I say this next part, you'll all probably throw things at me, but I think we take money from the tourism budget to give to these kids. One less festival could do it, and honestly, shouldn't our kids, the future of Sunrise Bay, be more important than someone who travels here once a year?"

There are a lot of grumblings and whispers. Gavin's eyes find mine and I want to tell him I agree with him, because I've been saying that for years. We spend way too much on tourism and not enough on our own residents. Yes, tourism helps to support the families in town, but there are other ways to do it without spending so much money on traditional print ads, posters, and such. A good social media campaign can draw people in, and I have a lot of other ideas. Sometimes small towns like to keep doing things one way because that's how it's always been done.

Hell, we've had an unfinished hotel sitting vacant for years when we could've torn it down and used the land for something else. But I'll never go against my mom and tell Gavin how I feel. And from the hushed tones in the auditorium, I'm not sure that many people agree with him anyway.

For the rest of the night, many of the questions go the same way. Mom gives the answers the townspeople want to hear, and Gavin says things that are so opposite, so outside of the realm of anything Sunrise Bay has ever done, I think he might've just lost his campaign all on his own.

But at the end of the night when I'm helping to put away chairs, there's still a line of people waiting to shake his hand, so maybe I'm wrong. But I don't think I am.

What surprises me is that minutes after everyone's gone, he's next to me, waiting to put a chair on the cart.

"Want to take me on a tour of your high school?" he asks. I open my mouth, but he's quick to add, "I'm coming in tomorrow to talk to some of the kids and I don't want to look like a loser and get lost."

"And you expect me to help you?"

"I'm asking for your help. I don't expect it." The look on his face already has me agreeing. "I'll trade you one haircut."

"Well then. Allow me to be your tour guide."

Chapter Twelve

Gavin

I should've stacked the chairs and gone home, but I wasn't ready to leave Posey yet.

"Once I finish sweeping the floors, I'm locking up," the custodian tells us.

"Thanks, Al." Posey waves to him as we walk out into the hallway of the high school. "Do you miss your high school days so much that you want to relive them tomorrow?" she asks, never looking at me.

My hands are in my pockets, hers linked behind her back. "I never went to high school."

She nods. "Homeschooled?"

"All of us from *High Society* had school on the set for a few hours every day. Sometimes we got to miss if they were shooting a big scene. Honestly, we all passed whether we actually did pass or not. Sad really."

"This is the English wing." She points down the hallway. "Science." Her finger moves to another hallway in the opposite direction. "There are only two stories and mostly it's all classrooms upstairs."

I stop at a glass case and if I didn't know the Greene name was big in Sunrise Bay, I'd know it after looking here. It's shoved full of trophies and pictures of Cade, Jed, Fisher, and Adam. A bigger display of Xavier Greene, pro quarterback for the San Francisco Rebels, sits in the middle.

"Isn't that Cade's wife?" I point at a picture from a school dance next to a newspaper article about Xavier committing to a D1 college.

She laughs. "No. That's Clara, Xavier's... well, they were best friends since they were young, but now I don't know what they are. They don't seem to be talking. She's Cade's wife's sister. It's a long story I can tell you another time. Maybe." She shrugs, as though maybe there wouldn't be another time to tell me.

"And where are all the Posey Greene accolades?"

She huffs. "I didn't play football. Or any sport, for that matter."

"Theater?"

"Nope."

"Band?"

"No again. I didn't do clubs or sports. Just wasn't into any of that." She shrugs again. "Honestly, if my name weren't Greene, no one would've known me in this school."

"I find that hard to believe." I can't help the way my gaze dips down her body.

"It's true. Chevelle was the one all the guys wanted."

"That surprises me."

That's the truth. Chevelle seems great, but she seems like a bit of a party girl. Which, now that I'm thinking about it, might have seemed like easier pickings for a high school guy, rather than a quiet girl with deep thoughts like the woman in front of me now. Still, I have no doubt Posey had her share of admirers whether she knew it or not.

We continue walking. She points out the cafeteria, the auditorium, the office, the music room. When she's pretty much done with the tour, we walk back to the auditorium to grab our coats and belongings. Perfect timing, because Al is just finishing.

On the way down the hall to leave, I figure I've used every excuse I have to spend time with Posey, and I try to think of a way to keep her in my presence.

"Can I ask you a question?" Her voice is so quiet I barely hear her.

"Always."

"Why are you meeting with the kids tomorrow?"

"You mean because they can't vote?" I chuckle and she joins me, nodding.

"Yeah."

"Because they're the best ones to tell me what needs to change around here. The youth is our future. They have their own perspective."

I open the door for her to exit and find that the weather is warmer than it's been at night in weeks. It's still coat weather, which I've come to love. At first when I moved here, I thought I'd miss the LA weather, but I don't at all.

"And you really believe that we should take from the tourism budget and give to the schools?"

"I do. I understand that tourism is how Sunrise Bay survives and I'm not saying it's not important, but we have to take care of ourselves too. The youth have to have the same advantages as other kids. If they don't, then what's the point? I just think we should come first. And by we, I mean the residents."

She doesn't say anything for a moment, and I figure, like a lot of Sunrise Bay lifers, she probably hates the idea.

"It's the opposite philosophy from my mom's," she says. "She believes in making tourism priority number one."

I nod, lips pressed together. "I know."

I saw her reaction to my answers at the debate. She

thinks that this mayor thing isn't important to me. Which is fine, because I love to prove people wrong. The casting director who said I was nothing special. The agent who wouldn't take me on after *The Carters* because I'd never be a heartthrob. Everyone thought of me as the little adorable kid with snappy comebacks.

"It's a unique outlook no one before you has had. I'm interested to see it pan out." She smiles and walks toward her car. "Good luck, Price."

I follow her, and both of our hands land on the handle of her door at the same time. "Please, allow me." My voice is gruffer than normal.

She stares at me for an uncomfortable minute, then her hand slides out from under mine. "Thank you."

"You know, Posey, I—"

She shakes her head. "Don't say it. We're on opposite sides now, and maybe that will change in the future, but right now, you're my enemy."

I shake my head. "That's crazy."

"Is it though?" Her head tilts. "You're standing in the way of what my mom wants. I'm sorry, but that puts you here." She holds out her left hand, then her right hand comes up. "And me here." We're as far apart as her arms will reach.

I nod, stepping back from her car. "Have a good night."

"Good night, Gavin."

I watch from a few footsteps back as she starts her car and pulls out of the parking lot.

"That woman's an enigma," Al says from beside his beat-up Chevrolet.

"Excuse me?"

"You're not the first guy to try to figure her out. Those Greenes... something sets them each back. Whether it's Hank's or Marla's kids, you gotta get through their hard exterior before you're rewarded. I've seen many guys fail because of a lack of trying or giving up, just as they would have won. Sad really. Tread carefully." He gets into his pickup truck.

What the hell? He acts as if the Greenes are a different species.

I haven't shied away from much in my life except for the press. I'm not going to start now.

I finish my run and see two missed calls. A long time ago, I decided I didn't care whose call I missed, my runs are for me, and I wouldn't sacrifice that time.

"Loved your thoughts at the debate," Fran calls to me. She and her three friends are on the park bench.

Does it creep me out that they watch me with such intent? Hell yes, but they seem harmless.

"Thank you, ladies." I wink and they each sigh.

I learned a long time ago I might not like having that effect on someone, but I have no control over it. Five years ago, I tried the whole scruffy face with unruly long hair thing. The more unkempt I became, the more attractive people thought I was. I was named sexiest man by *People* magazine that year.

I press my voice mail button, already knowing what to expect. I've been dragging my feet on contacting my agent, Darby.

"Gav, you have to return my phone call. People are calling for you, wanting you to audition. They don't care about the rehab thing. You're one of many, just like I told you. Call me today please."

I sit down on the grass hill, staring at the bay, drinking my water. I need to send her the termination paperwork, which will mean paying her for ending my contract early. When I signed the one-year contract four months ago, I thought I could do it—go back to acting. But my first gig after rehab proved I was over it. But if that's the truth, why haven't I sent the termination paper back and ended it for good?

The next message plays. "Sweetie, it's Mom." As if I didn't know. "Darby called looking for you. Please tell me you're safe. If you're in a bad way, come home. It's okay. Please just call Darby. I love you, sweetie. Bye."

The fact it took a call from my agent for her to worry whether I'm passed out in a ditch or high on pills reminds me of where my parents' loyalty lies.

Standing, I pocket my cell phone and turn to go home to shower before heading to the high school, but I freeze when I see Posey outside the inn. Her sister Mandi is at her side and they're talking. Posey's head falls back in laughter.

She's so beautiful. I wish I was the guy who could show her that. But the harder I push, the further I feel her pull away. Hopefully, one day she'll find a guy who treats her as special as she is. Who worships her body, whispering how amazing she is. Someone to hold her hand as they stroll through downtown, showing her off because he's the lucky bastard who got her.

Too bad that guy won't be me.

I trudge up the hill, knowing I should go another way. What can I say? I suck at listening to my inner self. So instead of heading home for a protein shake and a shower, I'm suddenly being shown to a table on the terrace of the restaurant at the inn so I can have breakfast.

Posey spots me immediately, her cautious eyes following me as I weave through the tables to where the hostess seats me. Mandi follows her sister's vision and smiles over her shoulder at me.

"Good morning, Gavin. I see your fans didn't disappoint." Mandi nods toward where Fran and her gang sit and laughs at her own joke.

"Haven't missed a day yet." I shift my vision to Posey. "Posey." I nod.

"Gavin." She's sitting on a chair and her knees are up to her chest, coffee resting between her hands.

"Sit here, Gavin. I have to head back in anyway." Mandi stands before I have a chance to sit at my table.

"I was going to leave too." Posey's feet fall to the ground.

"No, you weren't. Please, Gavin. Take my seat. I'll send Ellis over." She leaves us, ignoring the death glare from her sister.

"I don't have to," I say, my hand on the back of Mandi's vacant chair.

Posey exhales with a huff. "It's fine. Being the youngest, I'm not really good with being by myself anyway." Her arm extends for me to sit down. "Get a soufflé. You won't regret it."

"Done." I never open the menu.

The cutest smile crosses her lips, like she likes that I trust her opinion that much. "So, when am I cutting your hair?"

I run my hand over my sweaty head. "Is Friday cool? With the pancake banquet on Saturday, I want to be picture ready."

She chuckles and brings her legs back up to her chest, resting her coffee between her hands again. "What it must be like to be Gavin Price."

Her tone suggests it would be wonderful, but she has no idea. If I could disappear and have no one remember me as an actor, I'd give up everything it gave me. But that can't happen, so I have to live this life in what half the time feels like a foreign body.

"What must it be like to be Posey Greene?" I ask in return, hoping to keep the attention off myself.

She scoffs. "Boring." She raises her eyebrows.

"What?"

"One word. Tell me what it's like to be Gavin Price in one word."

Ellis comes over, and the distraction gives me time to think after I order a coffee and soufflé. Posey talks to her a little bit, but once Ellis leaves the table, Posey's eyes find mine. She doesn't voice her question again, but her green eyes make it clear she's waiting for my answer.

"Drained," I answer honestly.

Her smile tips to a frown. This is exactly why I like to keep the topic of conversation off of me. "I don't believe that."

I lean over the table. "And I don't believe one ounce of you is boring."

"Maybe you just need to relax. A massage might do you good," she says.

"Are you volunteering?"

Her expression doesn't change, but her cheeks pinken. "I'm your hairdresser. The massaging stops at the scalp."

"Have I told you how much I love it when you wash my hair?"

"No, but the sexual noises you make give it away."

I almost spit out my coffee but manage to swallow it. "I think we're actually building a friendship here," I say once I recover.

"You shouldn't think so much," she says, but she chuckles.

God, how will I ever break this woman?

Chapter Thirteen

Posey

I've never been a fan of the pancake banquet, especially when I volunteer to help out. It's held in the high school cafeteria, and you have to buy tickets for certain time slots, which means I'm here all day when I would usually be making money at my salon. I'm opening up tomorrow to make up for not working today.

I put on my Vote Greene pin, leaving my mom at her booth in the corner of the room. Although if I know her, she'll be everywhere but there all day, probably passing out pancakes as well.

Naomi Needles approaches as I finish adding plates of pancakes to my tray. "Where's Gavin Price?"

"Not my day to let him out of the cage," I say and walk away, but her heels click on the linoleum behind me.

"Come on. He's supposed to be here, right?"

"I don't know, Naomi. Why?" I glance over my shoulder at her.

We went to high school together. She married and divorced her high school sweetheart when he decided he wanted to move up north to a more remote territory to live off the grid. She stayed here and is raising their three-year-old daughter. These days she hangs around with a whole gaggle of young moms.

"Because we want pictures. I've been trying to track him down for weeks."

"Track him down?" I place some pancakes in front of the people, patiently waiting. "We're in Sunrise Bay. The town isn't that big. Where exactly are you looking?"

She twists her face into annoyance and shakes her head at me. "I'm not an idiot."

"Never said you were."

"From what I hear, he always seems to be around you. Even if you cut him."

"Don't believe everything Nikki says." I head back toward the kitchen to grab another tray, trying to lose her, but she hangs on like a trained K-9.

"Are you guys dating?" Naomi leans forward, but I slide between two chairs so she can't get side by side with me.

"He's campaigning against my mom."

"Okay, so he's available then?" She turns toward her group of moms sitting at one of the tables and gives them a thumbs-up.

There are no pancakes ready, so I have no choice but to wait. "Are you guys going to propose a group sex thing?"

Naomi scoffs. "Seriously, Posey?"

"So they're just your cheerleading squad?" I voice my second guess, and the snarkiness in my tone is clear, even to me. This is not jealousy I'm feeling. It's just annoyance at Naomi because I never liked her.

"No, we just wanted to make sure he's available. Which, thanks for the info."

She's cute in her tight jeans and short sweater that shows off how having a kid hasn't affected her figure. Her hair is curled and her makeup is done perfectly. I don't have a three-year-old and I can't look that good.

Lucky for me, a round of applause steals her attention

and I turn to see her little groupie corner cheering because Gavin just walked in. He's wearing jeans and a black V-neck T-shirt that says Vote Price across his chest. He lifts his arm in a wave and Naomi is instantly gone from my side, heading right over to Gavin's.

I groan and turn back to see if the pancakes are ready. This is the last place I want to be today.

"Naomi Needles," Adam says from behind the griddle. "She's been a thorn in your side all these years." He flips a few pancakes.

"What are you talking about?" Adam is the closest to me in age of my stepbrothers.

"Come on. You both liked that douche Anton Powers, remember?"

"I never liked him." Lie. I was in love with him. Secretly of course, because he was prom king to Naomi's prom queen. Now he's gutting his meals and surviving off the land. "Just give me the pancakes."

He laughs and puts them out for me to take.

"I can handle those." Gavin's next to me, his arms outstretched for the tray.

"So you can give them to your groupies?" I ask, holding the tray to my chest.

"Groupies?" He looks around. "Who?"

"I've got these. You can wait and get your own."

I walk away from him and pass around the plates, telling everyone to Vote Greene each time I put a plate down, but once I'm back at the cooking station, Gavin's there again.

"We're not having a competition," I inform him.

Erwin still crosses the street to the other side if he sees me coming ever since the 10K race. I glance over and see that Gavin's chained Erwin to the table with pins and fliers and signs for people to show their support for Gavin.

"I'm just helping," Gavin says.

"Nice of you to be here on time," I sneer.

Adam clears his throat, but he can go suck it. I'm sick of being the cute and friendly Posey Greene. This whole day blows. I don't want to see Gavin and Naomi flirting all morning.

"Yeah, I was up late and slept through my alarm." He exhales.

"Up late, huh?" Adam says with a raised brow.

Gavin cocks his head. "What are you implying?"

"Up late would suggest—"

"Here." I shove a tray at Gavin. "Go feed your groupies." I nod toward the crowd of women who now have Vote Price adorning themselves. Might as well write it in glitter on their foreheads.

"You know, if you're jealous—"

"Shut up, Adam!" I yell a little too loudly because a few tables glance over.

Adam just laughs at me.

I purposely go to the opposite side of the room to pass out pancakes, returning only when I have no choice. I time it so Gavin isn't at the kitchen too, but after a few trips, we end up next to each other at the pancake station once again.

"Can we hurry this up?" I ask Adam, who goes slower, his movements exaggerated and drawn out.

Gavin chuckles. "You okay?" Gavin asks me. "Seem a little high strung."

"You know there isn't a shortage of males in Alaska, right? Men outnumber the women here."

He gives me that confused expression. "I'm not following why that matters."

"Those women don't need to be fighting over you." I glance over his shoulder, and he does the same.

Naomi and two of her friends are staring at him. They smile and wave. Gavin waves back.

"Oh, I get it." Gavin nods to himself.

"You get what?" I watch Adam's movements, hoping he'll move faster.

"You're jealous."

Adam coughs out a laugh but stops when I give him the side-eye.

"You're crazy." I take the tray of pancakes that's finally ready, but Gavin doesn't wait for his, following me instead.

"Is it? I have no control over those women and whether they want to ogle me."

"Ogle?" I stop and turn toward him. "Full of yourself, are you?"

"What word do you want me to use?"

I pass out the pancakes, dropping plates on tables and murmuring vote Greene. Gavin's right behind me and he tugs on my arm to get me to stop.

"I don't want those women, Posey. You know the woman I want."

My cheeks heat and I look around. "I've got to go to the bathroom."

I beeline it out of the cafeteria until I reach the bathroom, then I take several deep breaths at the sink. Why would I be jealous? I'm the one pushing Gavin away, not the other way around.

"Get it together, Posey," I tell myself in the mirror.

Shaking off my irritation with Naomi Needles, I exit the bathroom and return to the pancake station to find my brother Jed there.

"You've been replaced," he says. "Go sit down and eat something. Maybe your blood sugar is low. You're acting like a lunatic."

I growl. "I am not acting like a lunatic."

"Just go take a break."

I stomp away and realize that Jed might have a point because there are a lot of eyes on me.

Naomi shouts my name and raises her hand. Her friends are all huddled together, and Gavin is in the middle. Each of them has a Vote Price button on their shirt, and some of them are holding signs like it's a photo booth.

I walk over and Naomi hands me her phone. "Will you take our picture?"

Looking over my shoulder, I see everyone behind me waiting for a scene to unfold. They probably think this will send me right over the edge into Crazyville. Gavin's face is full of concern and apology.

"I'd love to." I take her phone.

While I'm walking back and making sure I get everyone in the frame, Naomi is all up on Gavin. "What are you doing tonight? We were going to play cards at Ari's. Want to join? Don't worry, it won't be strip poker—"

"Ready?" I ask. "One. Two..."

"Unless you want to play strip poker," she finishes right as I say three.

I roll my eyes and purposely cut all their heads off in the picture. I hand the phone back to Naomi and walk away.

"Posey, the heads are cut off," she screeches behind me.

"Oops," I say, raising my hand and walking away.

My mom's gaze is on me the entire time I cross the room. I plop into the chair next to her. She picks up one of her signs and puts it in front of us to block us from anyone looking.

"Talk to me," she says.

I shake my head. "I'm fine. Just a bad day."

"Are you sure?" She rests her hand on my knee. "You can talk to me."

I doubt she wants to hear that I like Gavin Price. How he took me on an amazing date and then decided to run for mayor against her, which made him our enemy. Now my high school nemesis is flirting with him and it's pulling some horrible version of my personality out of me.

"It's just Naomi... you know we've never gotten along."

"I know. You two have a habit of falling for the same man." She rolls her eyes.

Who didn't know I liked Anton Powers? Jeez.

I pick up the sign and put it back in position. "I'll be fine. You have way too many pins here."

She laughs as I grab the basket. Plastering on a smile, I go to pass out some pins, purposely going to the tables with all the men, some of whom are the husbands of Gavin's groupies.

"Posey! Give me one of those." Ari's husband raises his hand. "Fucking Price. Does Ari forget how much she wanted me in high school?"

I laugh, and the rest of the guys ask for a pin too.

It's clear how this race is going to go down. If I can get my mom the men's votes, we should have the advantage. *Take that and your good looks, Gavin Price.*

I look across the room and find Gavin talking with four fishermen, who look as if they just got back from a long trip. He has them laughing and they seem receptive to him.

Hmm. Looks like it's not only the female vote Gavin can win over. Something has to be his kryptonite; I just have to find out what it is.

Chapter Fourteen

Gavin

"So this is the annual Sunrise Bay fest?" I soak in the experience. Families. Couples. Every age group from newborn to one hundred. A band plays on the big stage. It's literally something right out of the movies.

I'm at my booth that hasn't had much traffic. Everybody here wants to play games, ride the rides, and eat junk food. No one wants to stop by the mayoral candidate's booth and chat about zone regulations and budgets.

"Yeah." Erwin leans back in his folding chair, fiddling with his Rubik's Cube. He told me that it's his new obsession since he can't play video games when he's with me. I think maybe I'm way too lenient of a boss.

"And it happens every year?" I ask.

I feel pulled to go out with the masses and laugh and have fun, but my goal is to win this election. What kind of mayoral candidate plays games and gets his picture taken with powdered sugar all over his face from the funnel cake? Definitely not Arnold Schwarzenegger.

Ethel comes up to the booth. Her sidekick, Dori, is with her, as well as a brunette I don't know.

"You think you're going to get elected like this? You need to go out there and mingle." Ethel looks beyond me. "Surely Erwin can handle handing out pins. Right, Erwin?"

He straightens up in his chair as though he's a student and Ethel is the nun holding the ruler at a Catholic school. The Rubik's Cube slips out of his grasp and the dark-haired woman picks it up.

"Give Erwin back his toy, Midge," Dori says, taking it out of her hands and placing it on the table.

"I'm not sure," I say. "This way, I'll be sure to see everyone."

Ethel looks up and down the booths. "Hmm... strange that I don't see my daughter-in-law's tent. Do you think she's hunkered away from all the fun?"

Sure as shit, the woman is right.

Her gray eyebrows raise to her matching hairline.

"Let's go have fun," I say, stepping away from the table. "I'll bring you back some cotton candy, Erwin."

He's so busy fiddling with the Rubik's Cube he probably doesn't know I left.

The minute we're away from all the tents, Ethel stops and looks around. "Oh, look. There are my grandchildren." She hooks her arm with mine. "Would you mind walking me over? It's a little muddy and you wouldn't want to be responsible for me breaking a hip, right?"

Logan totally underplayed this whole Ethel and Dori fix up thing, but since I'm actually into a Greene—Posey Greene, to be exact—I'll gladly play along.

"Of course."

She pats my hand. "I knew you were a good man."

"Don't worry about us, not like I'm older than you or anything," Dori says.

Ethel looks over her shoulder. "Hold on to each other."

The ground isn't even muddy. Just a little soft from the evening rain yesterday.

"What is this festival for?" I ask Ethel on the way over to

the Greenes, who have positioned themselves in a little circle, eating and dancing with one another. Now here's a family that should have their own reality TV show.

"It signals the beginning of tourist season in Sunrise Bay. Gets them into town to spend their money. Get the towns-folk together before all the working folk are running off their feet until the season ends. The new mayor should know what's so special about it."

I smile at the elderly woman. "Do you think I could have coffee with you someday?"

"Coffee?" She looks unimpressed. "How about a night-cap?" Now she's smiling.

"That will work too. I've done a lot of research, but I'd like to talk to someone who's lived here longer. But I understand if you feel as though you're not being loyal to Marla."

She waves me off. "Honestly, Marla could win this race in her sleep. Everyone loves her. And me giving you information on Sunrise Bay back in the day isn't going to change that. I like the effort you're putting in. It's an admirable quality, but between me and you, you're going to lose."

I'm taken aback for a moment. "Not if I can help it."

She pats my hand. "And that's exactly the perseverance I want when it comes to winning over my granddaughter."

"What?" I say through a laugh.

"You don't fool me. I see it. I've seen it for a long time now, but we've chosen to wait and give you the opportunity to get your vices under control. Make sure you're in a good spot."

I stop and Dori curses, almost running right into my back. "You know?"

"Darling, everyone knows. It's nothing to be ashamed of. Especially with the environment you were brought up in. It's like an infestation, of course you were going to get bitten.

Look at you now. All healthy." Ethel pinches my cheek as though I'm that little kid on *The Carters* again. It aggravated me then, but now, not so much. "And believe me, not just anyone is good enough for my granddaughter."

"Thank you. I promise—"

"Promise me nothing. Just follow that heart of yours and you'll be fine."

We start walking again, and by the time we reach the group, Dori and Midge are already there. Midge is dancing in the middle of everyone. That woman seems like a bit of a loose cannon.

"Look who I found, everyone!" Ethel announces. For some reason, I thought I'd just slide in through the group and maybe corner Posey and ask her to join me on the Ferris wheel.

But now the whole group of Greenes turns to face me. Some of the women smile and wave, some of the guys nod. Posey turns back around to her niece, Emilia.

The band playing says their time is up and that another band will be coming up in fifteen minutes.

"Hey." Logan comes over and grips my shoulder.

"Hi."

He laughs at my lack of enthusiasm. "What's up?"

"I'm supposed to be campaigning and here I am with a group of people who aren't going to vote for me. And the one person I was hoping to talk to by coming over here won't even look at me, so..."

"Just have fun. The Greenes know everyone. Let them introduce you."

I feel as though I'd be slighting Marla. "Where are Marla and Hank?"

"Hank wasn't feeling well, so Marla stayed home with him. Which reminds me." He looks out into the crowd of people. "We're in charge of Rylan. Give the kid room to breathe but not too much, you know? So if you see anything offside, let me know."

"It's a crazy age."

Logan and I talk for a while. Some of the brothers come over and shake my hand, being pretty cordial, what with their mom running against me.

"You're Gavin, right?" Presley's look-alike says to me. She puts out her hand, and I shake it. "Clara Harrison. Presley's sister."

"Nice to meet you."

She sips her beer. "You too. I kept meaning to approach you, but it just wasn't ever the right time."

"I remembered you as a brunette?" At least in the school picture with Xavier, she was. Now that she's a blonde, I see how much she and her sister really do look alike.

"Yeah, it felt like time for a change. I'm gonna find out if blondes really do have more fun."

She laughs before I can say anything to refute it. I swear seventy-five percent of the women in Los Angeles are blonde. Posey's red hair was such a refreshing change that it was a turn-on.

"It looks good."

"Thanks." She sips her beer again, and we watch the new band take the stage, setting up their equipment. "You'll like this band. All girls, Madonna cover band."

"Nice." I nod. I'm not all that into Madonna, but if she's excited, I'm not going to ruin her fun.

Posey keeps glancing in my direction, but she turns away the minute our eyes catch.

I talk with Clara for a few more minutes, mostly about her job as a librarian.

"I saw your picture in the high school picture case," I mention to try to break the ice even more.

A puzzled expression creases her features at first, but then she seems to know what I'm talking about and nods. "With Xavier?"

"Yeah, you two at some dance."

A small sigh escapes her. "Prom. That was a long time ago."

There's longing in her tone that makes my chest ache for her. I've never thought of myself as a perceptive person, but this girl is hurting and forcing on a smile for everyone else.

The band announces they're going to start, and the first song up is "Vogue." All the Greene women go crazy, cheering and screaming. Molly grabs Emilia to get her to dance with her.

"What? Don't get her hooked on this," Jed says.

"Sorry, babe, it's a rite of passage." Molly drags Emilia closer to the stage.

Mandi, Presley, Lucy, Nikki, and Allie follow shortly after at Clara's insistence.

Posey returns from getting a drink and hands it to her brother Jed. "Vogue!" she yells and jumps into the middle of the women, doing all the poses that are on the video.

The women show Emilia how to pose, and she's pretty damn cute as she raises her arms and juts her hip out when they all freeze. The men shake their heads with smiles, their hands overflowing with either babies, purses, or drinks while they watch. My gaze doesn't leave Posey or the way her hips sway in her tight jeans. Her long red hair swishes, and she has the biggest smile. I'd do anything to have my hands on her hips right now.

"Go join them." Ethel nudges me.

All the Greene men stare at me as though they're horrified by the idea of me going out there.

"No." I guffaw and shake my head.

"Why not?" She looks at her grandsons and grandsons-in-law. "Don't listen to them, they all did embarrassing stuff to win over the women they love."

I look at them and they all shrug and nod in agreement.

But I don't have a chance to protest again because Ethel seems to have someone on the inside working with her. Emilia comes up to me, grabs my hand, and pulls me to the dance floor, positioning me right next to Posey.

Again, seems Logan was right on the mark with this. I'm just thankful I want the same thing those two old women do.

As I resign myself to my fate, the song ends and the band plays "Crazy For You."

I stand there awkwardly, but every other guy comes out to dance with his wife, fiancée, or girlfriend. Leaving Posey, Clara, and Mandi on their own, which seems okay. I'm about to bolt, but before I can turn around, two men approach Clara and Mandi and ask them to dance.

I stare at Posey, and she starts to walk away. I lightly clasp her elbow, causing her to turn. The question is clear in her eyes—why would we do this?

I lean closer to her ear. "It's only a dance."

Her eyes lock with mine and I can practically see her mind working. She looks away but eventually relents, allowing me to pull her into my arms. We start off with enough space to have another body between us, but eventually, I draw her closer. When she doesn't knee me in the nuts, I count it as a win.

I have no idea if things could work out for us, but this warm feeling in my chest from having her so close, the smell of her perfume, the glowing neon lights of the carnival rides shining down on us… I can't help but think something brought me here. Some force more powerful than me.

The words to the song are perfect for what I feel for her. As we sway, our eyes don't meet. Still, I've never felt more connected to someone.

As the song ends, I whisper in her ear, "I'm crazy for you."

She tips her head up to look at me. There's still so much doubt in her eyes, and it makes my heart pinch.

The band transitions to a fast-paced song, and Posey tries to leave, but I hold her in place.

"Come on a ride with me?"

She shakes her head. "Shouldn't you be campaigning?"

She's right. I should be shaking people's hands and trying to win them over, but right now, she's the only person I care about winning over. "Come on."

"I can't."

I look around, desperate to find some way of getting her on a ride with me, to have three minutes of alone time with her. "Then let's play a game. You pick the game, and if I win, you come on a ride with me."

She smirks and crosses her arms. "Fine. You're getting the shit end of the stick on this one, Price."

I follow her to the games area, watching her ass the entire way. God, she's got me following her like a dog with his tongue hanging out. Pretty soon, I'll need to remember where my priorities lie, or I have no hope of winning this election.

Chapter Fifteen

Posey

I've loved the carnival every year. But this year will go down as the best year yet. I danced with Gavin Price. Goose bumps still race down my spine when I remember him whispering that he's crazy for me. He's not holding back with his feelings and my willpower is slowly waning because the truth is... I want him too.

The problem is that he's my mom's competitor and I can't go against her. She's not even here tonight because she's taking care of Hank. She's always putting people's needs before her own.

"This is interesting," Jed says from behind me.

His daughter, my niece, comes alongside me. "I thought we were dancing."

She links her hand with mine. Emilia is the cutest thing ever.

"We're going to go play a game," I tell her.

Emilia's big toothy smile has me smiling in return. "I love games. Can I play?"

"Of course you can."

"Yay!"

I'm not sure why all my siblings are following me to the games section, other than pure nosiness. Nikki's probably jotting down notes to retell on her radio segment.

"What'll it be?" Gavin asks, his arms out to his sides in front of the row of games.

I walk over to the basketball game.

"I knew it. Pay up, Cade," Jed says.

"You should know that Posey thinks she missed her calling as a Harlem Globetrotter," Cade tells Gavin. "She'd play Around the World in the driveway all the time."

"You're just upset because she beat you." Mandi, my dear sister, sticks up for me. I give her a smile of thanks.

"Once. And when it came to one on one, she lost," Cade says.

"Because you're about six inches taller than her." Mandi, God help her, will defend me forever.

"All right, basketball it is then." Gavin cuts through all my siblings' bullshit and pulls out his wallet.

"Yep. You've played?" I ask.

He shrugs. "Hasn't everyone?"

I'm not sure I get what he means. I'm sure there are people who haven't played basketball, but whatever.

"What's the wager between you two?" Jed stands at the side of the game, leaning his shoulder on the edge. He ignores Emilia jumping around, asking when it's her turn.

"I win and Posey goes on a ride with me," Gavin says.

Jed laughs. "I guess we know which ride he's taking you on."

"What ride?" Emilia asks.

He smooths his hand down her hair, tugging on a braid that Molly must've done.

"The Ferris wheel," every man in my family says in unison.

Gavin's cheeks turn red. If I wasn't supposed to dislike him, I'd think it was adorable.

"How come the Ferris wheel?" Emilia asks.

"Everyone takes their dates on the Ferris wheel with the hopes you get stuck on top and can sneak some..." Jed looks down at Emilia.

"Sneak what?" Her eyes are wide.

"Just to talk."

"Like you and Mommy talk sometimes?"

Everyone makes a sound knowing exactly what Molly and Jed are doing when they're "talking."

"Exactly, sweetie." Jed looks at me. "Let's get this over with."

Gavin puts down money for both of us.

"Oh no, I pay for myself." I dig into my purse and slap down a five-dollar bill.

"Is she always so difficult?" Gavin asks my siblings, and they all say yes in unison.

If Emilia wasn't floating around, I'd flip them off.

We're each given a basketball and Gavin holds his, turning toward me, putting his arm out for me to go first. "Ladies first."

I inhale a deep breath. I was always good at basketball, and this is the only game I have any chance of winning. There was no way I was going to choose throwing a ball to down a pyramid of something, or darts to break balloons.

I bounce the ball on the ledge and stare at the hoop. It looks really far away now. I throw the ball and it comes off my fingertips, circles the hoop, but doesn't go in.

"That's okay, you got this," Mandi says, coming to my side. She looks past me at Gavin. "Best two out of three, right?"

He lifts a shoulder. "Sure."

The guy hands me back the basketball and I do my usual ritual, except this time I push away all the pressure of everyone watching me. I shoot the ball and it bounces off the backboard into the net.

"Yes!" Mandi screams and picks up Emilia, who is just as excited. "One more, Posey."

Instead of waiting for the guy to hand me the ball, Gavin offers me his. I accept and our fingers brush during the exchange. I'm reminded that I might not mind going on a ride with him, but I just can't admit it to myself.

"Thanks," I say.

He nods.

I bounce the ball on the ledge and shoot the ball, sinking it in the net.

"Way to go!" Mandi yells.

Emilia squirms to get out of her hold. "My turn!"

Jed says, "Not yet. Gavin goes first."

We all look at Gavin, who doesn't seem at all fazed about me making two baskets.

"Great job," he says to me and accepts the ball from the guy working the game.

With both hands on the ball, he spins it, then bounces it on the ledge in a way that says this isn't the first time he's held a basketball. An exhilarating rush fills my stomach. Damn traitor.

He shoots the ball and sinks it.

"Looks like Gavin didn't just act growing up," Cade says from behind us.

I turn and narrow my eyes at my stepbrother.

"Lucky throw," Gavin says, winking at me.

Bullshit.

Gavin does the whole spin-y thing again and sinks the second shot. I might as well accept my defeat and get ready to sit my ass in the Ferris wheel. Although maybe it will be nice to be all the way up there with no prying eyes.

Nobody says anything as he's handed the ball for the third time. He does his same ritual, but this time he stares at me when he shoots. It's such an arrogant, egotistical thing to do and it should not turn me on, but who am I kidding? I feel heat pulsing from my head to my toes.

"Not much to do on a set between takes. We played basketball." Gavin shrugs as though it's no big deal.

I picked the game, it's not like he hustled me, so I decide to be a good sport.

"Fine, let's go get this over with." I head in the direction of the Ferris wheel.

"Actually, that's not my choice."

I look from him to my family, who seem surprised.

"Tilt-A-Whirl," he says, taking my hand and walking me in the opposite direction.

"Game changer," Jed jokes and all my siblings laugh at my expense.

Lucky for us, though, none of them follow us to the ride. I guess maybe they can tell when their presence isn't wanted.

We wait in line for the Tilt-A-Whirl, along with every kid and the parents who have to ride because their kids don't reach the minimum height to ride alone. No sane adult wants to go on the Tilt-A-Whirl.

"No spinning, okay?" I say to Gavin.

"That's the fun of the ride."

"Let it spin on its own. We don't need to add more to it."

He says nothing, so I think he's not going to honor my request. That seems to be the trend with him.

We walk through the metal gated area and Gavin takes us to the back blue bin. Allowing me in first, he follows and secures us in our seat, bringing the bar down. He jokingly uses his hips to spin us. I narrow my eyes at him, and he laughs.

"It's funny," he says, his fingers running over the metal bar. "You didn't fight me on this too hard."

"Well, you won. I pay my bets in full." I'm honest, even though I have a feeling if I'd won at basketball and he still asked, I might've gone on a ride with him anyway. Just not this one.

"Is that how I need to get you to do things with me? Bet you?"

I throw my hands in the air. "Okay, I give up. Why are you pursuing me when there's no chance?"

Confusion laces his beautiful features. "Why isn't there a chance?"

"Because it's a lose-lose situation. If you win the race, I can't prance you around my family and rub it in my mom's face. If you lose, you won't want to be around my mom. That is, if the mayor position is that important to you."

He slides along the seat to my side. "How can you continue to deny this?" He motions between us. "I've never in my life felt like this for a woman. I saw how jealous you were at the pancake breakfast."

I shake my head. "I was not jealous. Naomi Needles and I have history."

He nods and his arm goes around my shoulders. "Well, I have no interest in her. I've done what people wanted me to my entire life. I'm done with that. Now I want to take something for myself."

"That being?"

"Do you really have to ask?" His gaze falls to my lips and suddenly the confines of this blue shell feel suffocating.

"I can't," I barely whisper.

His fingers dip into my hair, his thumb brushing along

my cheek. "You can. You're choosing not to. Put yourself first, Posey. I promise it's going to feel amazing."

He lowers his head and oh boy, he's going to kiss me. I slide my tongue out to wet my bottom lip. I should stop him. I should. But the closer he gets, the harder it is to deny that he's right—I want this.

The ride starts with a jolt, but my awareness whittles down only to the feel of his lips on mine.

He kisses me with a softness I didn't anticipate. After a moment of hesitation, I slide a little closer to him, offering myself up. He groans and I whimper, raising my hand to touch his face. His five o'clock shadow prickles my palm. The softness of his hair threads through my fingers. This is what I've dreamed about for weeks—years, if I'm being honest with myself.

I'd imagined my mind would be screaming that I'm kissing Gavin Price, Hollywood heartthrob, but I'm not giddy because of that. In fact, I'm giddy because I'm kissing Gavin Price, Sunrise Bay resident. A man who's winning me over with the type of perseverance women dream about.

He strips his mouth from mine, his thumb sliding down the column of my throat. "Posey, you have no idea what you do to me," he says softly. "You drive me mad in the best possible way."

I giggle and my finger runs down his chest, feeling the abs I've only seen on display during his runs. I'm going to take this right now because it feels right. To hell with the consequences. I grip his shirt and tug him toward me, and a smile creases his lips before his mouth descends on mine again.

We're lost in one another until the ride slows, but our container continues to spin. I back up from him, nausea overwhelming me. I might have been caught up in our kiss, but it seems my body was well aware of the ride.

"You look pale," he says, reaching for me.

I look to the outside, where I catch a glimpse of Emilia waving at me.

"Oh god," I squeak.

Then I throw up all over Gavin.

The ride slows to a stop, and I stare at him, unsure what my next move is. He's looking at his lap in disbelief.

"You should've taken me on the Ferris wheel like a normal guy would have!" I free myself from the ride, embarrassment coating me.

If anything were to happen between us, which it can't, imagine telling my grandchildren, "Grandma threw up on Grandpa after their first kiss."

I'm such an idiot. I knew nothing good could come from involving myself with Gavin. This just proves it.

I rush off the ride and out of the carnival.

Gavin

$\mathcal{A}$ school board meeting isn't exactly the way I want to spend my Friday night, but I do want to win the mayoral race, so here I am.

"Have you seen my Rubik's Cube?" Erwin asks me from the passenger seat.

He didn't have to come with me tonight, I'd actually prefer he didn't, but he said he was bored.

"No."

"I haven't been able to find it in almost a week. I had it at the festival and now I can't find it."

"I don't know where it is," I say, annoyance leaking into my voice that has nothing to do with Erwin or his Rubik's Cube.

I'm on my last inch of rope with Posey. I'm clearly a lunatic because all I wanted to do after she threw up on me was take care of her, but she left me in a Tilt-A-Whirl with vomit-soaked clothes and she's been dodging me ever since. I texted her to see if she was okay and she replied with a simple yes. I went into the salon, and she pretended she had to get some hair dye from the back and never returned. I waited for fifteen minutes.

Tonight? I'm sure she won't be accompanying her mom just so she doesn't have to see me.

I park my truck and climb out. The lot is pretty full. I've learned that almost every big event is held in the Sunrise Bay High School gym or auditorium. It was a little surreal the first time I came into this building. Even though I acted in a television show that was supposed to take place in a high school, it was filmed at a small Catholic college that had closed down. I don't know what it feels like to walk down the halls of your high school with real classmates and not just fellow actors.

"Is she going to be here tonight?" Erwin asks.

I know who he's asking about. He rarely refers to Posey by name as if he's afraid she'll pop up if he does.

"Your guess is as good as mine."

"Do you think you'll just give up on her?" Erwin asks.

"What do you mean?"

"Because she holds all that shit in from her dad cheating on her mom. Plus, she puts her family above everyone. It would take a lot for you to become the priority over them. As your friend, I feel like I should set you straight—you won't win her."

I don't consider Erwin a friend, I consider him an employee, but he's being truthful. I wonder if I've been blind, seeing what I wanted to see. "We all have shit from our past."

"Yeah, but she holds on to hers like it's a life jacket."

"You're telling me you have nothing traumatizing from your childhood?" I have to think a guy who is only concerned about his Rubik's Cube and so easily gave up his blog about video games so he can be my assistant is harboring something.

"Sometimes you just have to say fuck it." He shrugs. "That was my life, and it sucked, but I made it through. I'm here now."

His statement feels oddly perceptive coming from Erwin.

"The past can still stop you from doing things, even if you think of it like that." I open the doors to the high school, kind of wishing he'd brought this up at a different time when we could dive deeper into it.

I walk into the room that's now buzzing with activity. Mostly everyone is near a refreshment table. Little groups of people mingle throughout the space, but it's a red-haired woman who catches my eye. Posey's talking with a guy about her age.

I elbow Erwin. "Do you know him?"

"Of course I know Hank Greene," Erwin says as if I'm the idiot.

"Not him. The guy Posey's talking to."

He leans forward like a ninety-year-old, squinting to get a look. "Shit, I didn't hear that he was back in town. That's Eli Easton. He and Posey..." He doesn't finish his sentence. "I'm gonna ask around about my Rubik's Cube."

Erwin moves to walk away, but I grab the back of his jacket and tug him back to my side. "He and Posey what?"

"You sure you wanna know?" He's all nervous energy, his weight shifting from foot to foot, his hands clenching and unclenching.

"Yes." I look back at her.

God, it's like a hammer to the heart. He just made her laugh. I want to be the one to do that to her. Now she's touching his arm. This is heart-wrenching. Is this how she felt when we were at the pancake breakfast?

"It's all rumor, but I mean, this is Sunrise Bay. Not a lot of liars around."

"Spit it out, Erwin," I snap.

"Eli was her first *real* boyfriend."

"Fuck," I murmur, reading between the lines. "Seriously? They dated?"

"Kind of. I think maybe. I wasn't in Posey's circle. I don't know the specifics. But rumor was that they were pretty hot and heavy for each other." He moves his head side to side like I don't have to believe him but it's probably true. "Then he left for college. Posey stayed. He's been gone for years. Heard he was going to be a doctor or something."

"Damn, is he the one who got away? Maybe it's not her dad who's messed her up, but this idiot who left her." I don't realize I'm talking out loud until Erwin answers.

"Your guess is as good as mine," he says. "Can I go search for my Rubik's Cube now?"

"Yeah." I run a hand through my hair and step forward to approach them, but I'm stopped by a blonde jumping in front of me.

"Hey, cutie," Naomi Needles says, her fingers trailing up the buttons on my shirt.

I step back and her hand falls to her side. "Hi, Naomi," I say and notice her pin. "Like the pin?"

She plays with it, her nails perfectly manicured and painted a bright red. "I told you I'm your gal."

"Thank you for the support. If you'll excuse me." I look over her shoulder at Posey to make sure she's still there.

Naomi follows my line of sight and chuckles. "Eli Easton is back, and he's definitely grown up. I'm sure Posey's playing the what-if game over there."

One thing is certain—I do not like or trust Naomi.

"Did Erwin tell you how hot and heavy those two were back in high school? Posey was crushed when he left." She shakes her head and sips from her Yeti cup, which I doubt has water in it. "He's back in town as a single father now. Probably trying to convince Posey to give him another chance." She turns to block me from seeing the two of them. "Who cares about them anyway? What are you doing after this boring meeting?"

"Going home. Now please excuse me." I slide past Naomi and walk over to where Posey and Eli just were, except they aren't there anymore. I look around, not spotting them.

What the hell? Where could they have gone?

Someone comes on the mic and asks everyone to be seated. Jesus, I haven't even tried to introduce myself to people. I'm really sucking on this campaign thing.

I find a seat in the back, spotting Eli showing Posey to a seat in the front. His hand is on the small of her back. I'm not a violent man, but I wouldn't mind breaking that hand off from the rest of his body. Possessiveness hijacks my mind.

The school board members are all lined up across the front, passing a microphone back and forth. They talk about a crosswalk where people are speeding and debate shifting it for the kids to cross farther down the road. I have no idea why that's safer, but everyone agrees, so it's nice that it's amicable.

They talk about the senior's gift of a park bench this year, then the budget for technology depending on the upcoming election, to which a few faces turn to me either disgusted or enthusiastic. Last, they try to decide whether a new elementary school should be built in the coming years, and I'm floored when I hear the reason why.

"The Greene children are starting to get married and having kids. We should prepare for an influx of children."

I bark out a laugh because how many kids can they have to require a whole new school? Everyone turns to me, and I quickly shift it to a cough, getting up to grab a water from the refreshment stand. Sometimes this town is too small.

Since there are varying viewpoints, the new school topic is suspended until the next meeting. The next topic is some classes they'd like to offer to the adults in the community. Fran and Nora agree to teach knitting, and someone else offers up a cooking class. But the only one that grabs my attention is when Eli Easton's hand flies up in the air.

"May I suggest one I think I'd benefit from?" he says.

"Eli, we heard you were back in town. Welcome." The woman leading the meeting offers a sweet smile.

"Thanks. Now that I've become a single dad, I need to figure out how to do girl hair. I wondered if someone like Posey could head a class like that." He looks at her when she scoffs. "Not to put you on the spot or anything."

The one cheek of Posey's I can see is bright red.

"That's a great idea. Jed could have used this, and I know we have a lot of new dads around town. There's a surge of new energy around Sunrise Bay." The same woman smiles proudly. "What do you say, Posey?"

"Um…" I hear reluctance in Posey's tone. She doesn't want to, nor does she probably have the time for it. "Sure. But I'll have to bring the woman who taught me everything —my mom."

"Perfect. We'll add that to next week's classes then." The woman jots it down in her planner.

An hour later, the meeting is over. It wasn't as painful as I thought it would be. Except for the part where I had to watch Eli lean over and whisper shit in Posey's ear.

I stay where I'm seated, pretending I'm on my phone and waiting for Posey to pass me. She does minutes later, Eli still at her side. As soon as she's two rows away, I stand, and she runs right into me. I place my hands on her shoulders to stop her from falling.

"Oh, Gavin, I didn't see you," she says.

Because this guy has demanded her attention all evening.

I put out my hand. "Gavin Price."

"I know." He shakes my hand firmer than necessary, as though he knows I'm a threat to him having Posey. "Eli. You're running for mayor? Loved you in *The Carters*."

This is how he's gonna play this? *The Carters*? Give me a fucking break.

"Can I talk to you for a minute, Posey?" I ask.

She stares at me for a moment until we have to move over, since a lot of people are trying to leave and groaning that we're in their way.

"I'm sorry, not tonight, Gavin. I had a really long day, so I'm just going to go home."

Damn her if she thinks she's going to continue to dodge me.

"It'll only take a second."

Eli puts up his hand. "You heard her."

I narrow my eyes at him.

Posey looks at him and puts her hand on his to lower it. "It's fine. Nice to see you, Eli, see you next week at the class."

She walks away and I follow her like a damn puppy.

Once we're by ourselves, she turns to me. "What can't wait, Gavin?"

"The fact that you're dodging me."

"I'm not dodging you, I'm simply busy. I've been neglecting my clients, and my mom needs my help."

"I want to talk about that kiss," I say, inching forward.

She looks around the room and puts her hand on my chest, searing me with the heat of her palm. "It was a mistake. I apologize, I don't want to play games with you. It was a momentary lapse of judgment."

"But this Eli guy is going to win you?"

Her eyebrows shoot up. "Win me? I had no idea I was like a stuffed animal in one of those claw games. Tell me, am I just hanging out on top or am I wedged between a stuffed pig and a stuffed bear?"

I exhale loudly. "You know what I mean."

She steps to the side, and when I match her step, her eyes bore into mine. "No, because I'm not something to play tug-of-war with. Have a great night, Gavin."

She walks away and I watch her go. One thing I can smile about is that she blows off Eli too.

"Bad news, boss, no one has seen my Rubik's Cube," Erwin says.

Jesus, Erwin. I have way bigger problems than a Rubik's Cube.

Posey

"Mom, I do not want to do this class. Spend my Saturday evening teaching dads how to braid hair?" I whine on our way to the high school. "You've seen Emilia. It's been months and her hair is still lopsided on the days Molly can't do it. Nothing I show them here tonight is going to help."

Mom blows out a breath, putting on her windshield wipers because of the light sprinkling of rain.

"This is a good thing and something Gavin can't be a part of. I thought that would make you happy at least." She glances at me with a smirk that clearly suggests she sees what's been going on between us.

"Don't give me that look," I say.

"What look? I'm not giving you a look." She smiles, her hands at ten and two, staring out the window.

"I knew I should've driven myself." I lean back in the seat and cross my legs.

"You don't have to talk to me about him, but I'm not blind."

I turn up the radio. She turns it back down, using the button on her steering wheel.

"What?" I ask.

"I just want to make sure you're not refusing to go out

with him because of this mayor thing. I'm more than okay with it if he makes you happy."

"And if he wins?" I ask.

She shrugs. "So be it. If he wins, then that's what was supposed to happen. It means I'm meant for something else."

"How can you be so casual about it? This job should be yours, Mom. Why does he think he can just come in here and take that from you?" My voice rises as the rain comes down harder, pounding on the roof.

"Whoa, sweetie, calm down. He isn't taking anything away from me. There must be some reason he wants to be mayor. Have you thought about asking him?"

"No," I say with a tone that implies that'd be absurd. "Why would I do that?"

"Because the minute you saw that Vote Price sign, you put a bulls-eye on him, but you're the only one with the arrows, sweetie. And when you aren't looking at him like you want to kill him, your eyes are filled with hearts. You're at war with yourself and I don't like it."

I stare out the window, my finger following a drop of rain that slips down the glass. "It's just a childhood obsession. Like if Paul McCartney came to Sunrise Bay, you'd be all gaga over him."

"First of all, you're aging me. Maybe if Jon Bon Jovi came to town." She chuckles. "But I married my childhood crush. I'm good."

I glare at her.

"The second one," she clarifies.

Phew, because she married my dad young and knew him in high school too.

She touches my leg before placing her hand back on the

steering wheel. "I really wish you'd explore things with him."

"Mom!" I cross my arms. "He's the enemy."

She parks in the high school parking lot and stays in her seat. This was her move when we were younger and we were fighting. We were told never to part ways while mad, so no matter what happened, we stayed in the car until we could talk it out.

"Gavin Price is not our enemy. He's just trying to find his place in the world."

"Says you."

What I won't say out loud is that I kind of agree with her. I've never asked him why he wants to become mayor. I assume it's because he wants to be another big name somewhere. If he hated the limelight like he says, why wouldn't he go bury himself in the woods somewhere like Naomi's ex-husband?

"I will work at being nicer," I say begrudgingly.

"Thank you. If I'm going to win, I can't have people giving him a sympathy vote because of my daughter." She laughs. "This is Sunrise Bay, sweetie, and there's no room for negativity because when this mayor race is over, we have to respect the town's decision no matter which way they voted."

She has a point.

"Okay," I murmur as I open the door to make a run for it through the rain and into the school.

Before I can get out, Gavin's Bronco peels into the parking lot, splashing a huge puddle on our car. I glare at him, then look at my mom.

She laughs. "Remember your brothers and how crazy they are."

"Why is he here?" I snipe, reaching for my bag in the back seat, then getting out of the vehicle.

I watch him get out of his truck. Erwin comes out the other side.

The four of us end up at the entrance at the same time. Other workshops are going on tonight, so surely Gavin's here to learn how to cook, or maybe he's going to go learn how to knit with Fran to score some brownie points.

"Why are you here?" I ask him as we step through the doors.

"To learn how to braid hair." He has a smile plastered on his beautiful face. I hate that his face makes me melt in appreciation even when I'm annoyed with him.

"You don't have kids," I say.

"Nice to see you two. I'm going to set up." Mom heads down the hallway.

Gavin nods in her direction. "Erwin, go help Mrs. Greene with her bags."

"She doesn't need help, Erwin, stay put," I say.

Erwin retraces his footsteps back to us.

"Go, Erwin," Gavin says and steps forward.

"Erwin, you take one more step and I will break that Rubik's Cube once you find it."

"Do you know where it is?" He comes face-to-face with me, sounding hopeful.

Gavin raises his eyebrows like I'm at fault for bringing it up in the first place.

"Sorry, I don't."

"Damn," he whispers.

I turn to Gavin. "You don't have kids. This is for fathers with kids."

He holds up his finger and all I want to do is bend it

backward until he's howling in pain. "Technically, it's just to learn how to do a kid's hair."

"And whose hair will you be practicing on?"

He takes off Erwin's skull cap. A flop of brown hair falls down to his shoulders. "Erwin."

"Seriously?"

"Don't worry, I washed it and dried it," Erwin says.

"Let's go, Erwin, we don't want to be late," Gavin says.

Erwin walks, but I tug on Gavin's sleeve, pulling him back to me. "What is your game?"

A devilish smile crosses his lips. "To make sure that Eli Easton doesn't get another shot with you."

The air leaves my lungs in a rush.

His smile deepens, and he walks away, leaving me speechless.

Our flirtation is one thing. The kiss we shared still haunts me late at night in bed. But now he's purposely going to keep me from being involved with someone else? Someone I wouldn't give another shot to if he was the last man in Sunrise Bay. But Gavin doesn't need to know that. In fact, I think I should play my own game.

I saunter into the room reserved for us and find Jed and Emilia already there.

"It's daughter/daddy night. Mommy is drinking wine," Emilia says to me. "She said one bottle might not be enough."

I run my fingers through my niece's thick hair.

Jed rolls his eyes. "Molly is making me come, even though I do a kick-ass job already. Right, kiddo?" He raises his hand, and she smacks it.

"Kick ass." Emilia grins.

Jed pulls her close. "That word stays between us, okay?"

Emilia nods, but I guarantee she'll say it again before she goes to bed tonight.

A few other dads and their daughters join us and then Eli walks in carrying a cute little girl with blonde hair, her head tucked into his neck. Mom approaches them first. I don't want to bombard the little girl, so I pass out the kits Mom put together that have a big sticker on top that says Vote Greene.

"Nice touch." Jed holds up one.

"Sorry, Erwin, I hope pink and purple are okay?"

"My favorite colors," he says, looking ridiculous sitting in the small chair in front of Gavin like the rest of the kids here.

I snicker from the absurdity of it all. Gavin really is pulling out all the stops.

Once Eli is seated, I wave to him, and he waves back.

"Can we get started?" Gavin says. "The weather and everything."

I narrow my eyes at his condescending grin, then I clap and announce that we're going to get started.

"Let's try a simple braid first. Can I borrow Emilia?" I ask my brother.

She's already walking toward me.

"Have at it. I already rock the braid," Jed says, and I roll my eyes.

I show the group how to split the hair into threes and weave it together. Once I have Emilia done, I tell her to go make her daddy try it on the other side. Then I go around the room and inspect how people are doing.

"It's just one over, then bring the other one over to that side and the same on the other side. Good job, Eli." I pat him on the back.

I compliment a few other dads who are definitely going to need some practice to master this.

"My hands just won't do that," Gavin complains when I make it over to him.

I go up behind him and touch Erwin's hair. It's so soft that it's slipping out of Gavin's fingers.

"Erwin, how much conditioner do you put in?" I ask.

"Half a bottle. I did a hot wax treatment too. Wanted my hair to be super soft for boss man," he says.

I nod and look at Gavin. "Okay, that's trickier for you."

I reach forward, my arms on either side of Gavin's neck. Damn, his cologne hits me and I'm back on that Tilt-A-Whirl again. The feel of his five o'clock shadow rubbing along my cheek, his sweet words of praise falling from his lips to my ear.

I pop my eyes open, trying to stay on task. My hands cover his and I manipulate them to do what I want them to do. Eventually, we manage to finish it and he ties off the braid with a small elastic rubber band.

"Perfect," I say and walk away so I can breathe again.

We do pigtails with the braids, which is super easy, but I do have to help most of the guys find the part and make sure it's a straight line down the middle. Mom takes over to explain the ponytail and some end up more on the right than the left, but they all pretty much ace it. They just need more practice.

"How about curling hair now?" I say. "Your little ones will be going places where you'll want them to look extra special."

"That's when I take her to her favorite aunt." Jed winks at me.

Mom laughs because to her, everything her son says is

funny. We're interrupted by her phone going off in her purse. She takes the call and heads out to the hall. Must be important.

"Who wants to volunteer?" I ask the room.

Eli and Gavin raise their hands at the same time.

"I'm not sure about the curling iron, Gavin," Erwin says, and the room laughs.

"Eli, come on up."

We try to situate his daughter in front of me, but she doesn't want to be up front. I look at Eli, not wanting to force the poor girl, and he nods, picking her up and taking her back to his seat.

"I guess that leaves Erwin," I say, forcing a smile.

He looks from Gavin to me. "Really?"

"It's fine. I'm not going to burn you," Gavin says as they both approach me at the front.

"You take one piece of hair and put it under the arm of the curling iron. Pull the curling iron down to the ends of the hair, then just turn it so it moves up the hair and twirls around." I demonstrate on my own hair, but I'll have to use Erwin as a model at some point. He has great hair for a guy. "Your turn."

I stand back, allowing Gavin to try it. Erwin's back is ramrod straight, as if he's prepared to bolt out of here at any moment.

I put a gentle hand on Erwin's shoulder. "It's easy for your child to fear the curling iron. It's hot and they can feel the heat when it's close to their head, but keep reassuring them they're okay, not to move and you won't burn them." I eye Gavin and he only stares at me as though I'm asking him to do an exorcism.

"Don't burn me, Gavin," Erwin says, and the room laughs again.

"Stop it. I won't, and even if I did, it can't be that bad," Gavin says.

I shake my head at him. "Not exactly the attitude you want to go in with."

Gavin takes a section of Erwin's hair, sticks it between the wand and the arm, but he doesn't get it right to the ends of the hair before winding it up, leaving Erwin with an indentation about an inch off his ends.

"It was a good try." I do another example on myself.

"Yeah, I think I'm done here." Erwin gets up and leaves.

Mom walks back in the room, and I know immediately that something is up. My entire body tenses.

"I'm sorry, but I have to go, everyone. Posey is going to finish up here. Thanks for coming and remember, vote Greene." Mom gives a wan smile in my direction.

I abandon the class and go over to my mom while she retrieves her purse. Jed is right behind me. Emilia wants to join us, but Gavin detours her, asking her what her favorite color is. Emilia responds with a very specific color of orange as I mouth thank you to him.

"Mom, is everything okay?" I ask.

"Hank isn't feeling well. It's nothing. I'll call you later." She looks at us and she's pale. There's definitely something she's not telling us. "You can get a ride?"

I nod. "I'll be fine. You go."

She kisses our cheeks and Emilia's several times before she's out the door and we hear her shoes clicking rapidly down the hallway.

Jed and I stare at one another, unsure what to do. Hank could just have the stomach flu or something, but Mom's face didn't look like it was something minor.

"Just keep going with the class. I'm sure she'd tell us if it was anything to be worried about," Jed says.

He's right. They've never hidden anything from us, not even when Mom got pregnant with Rylan.

I finish the class and give all the dads links to some online tutorials.

As I'm saying goodbye to Gavin and Erwin, Jed approaches me. "Hey, there's something I have to take care of at the brewery, so I gotta go. You got a ride?"

"I have her," Gavin says. "Do you mind taking Erwin? His car is back downtown."

"Sure." Jed kisses my cheek. "I'll let you know if I hear anything." He gives me a meaningful look and I nod.

I say goodbye to Emilia, then they're off.

"I can take you home if you need me to," Eli says when he comes over to say goodbye.

"I already told her brother I have it." Gavin stands between us, waiting for me. "You have your daughter, and she looks tired."

"Hungry," he mumbles.

I smile at the little girl who I'm pretty sure has her dad wrapped around her finger. She was fine when he wasn't touching her hair, but the minute he did, she'd whine, and he would stop.

"Yeah, you go, Eli. Thank you. It's a short trip for Gavin and I need to clean up and turn off the lights."

Eli looks at Gavin and back at me. "We should get together and catch up some time?"

Oh god, this is awkward.

"Sure," I say, not wanting to embarrass him in front of Gavin or his daughter, but hoping he forgets to pursue his idea.

Gavin growls, but Eli must not hear him because he smiles and picks up his daughter, then leaves. Once it's only

Gavin and me in the room, we pick up chairs and put them away, then I turn off the lights.

When we're in the hallway, Gavin smiles and swings his keys around his finger. "Where to?"

"Home," I say.

But I'm not prepared for what happens next.

Chapter Eighteen

Gavin

"Let me grab the truck and pull it up here," I tell Posey when we step outside the school and rain is pelting down past the overhang.

"I think I'm going to get wet either way unless you have an umbrella. Let's just run for it."

Posey sets off before I comprehend what she means. She doesn't use her hands to shield one drop of rain. I run after her and unlock the doors. Mine is the only car in the lot, besides the custodian who has to lock up the school behind us.

"It's cold," she says, but there's a light, fun tone to her voice.

I can't lie, my mind travels to every movie with a kiss in the rain. If Posey was mine and I didn't have to go to my side of the truck but to hers instead, I'd press her against the wet metal and take her in my arms. I yearn to know what our bodies would feel like together, the rain falling in sheets between our faces as I kiss her like I could never get enough.

Sadly, she opens the passenger door and slides in before I can even decide whether it's worth the risk to try out my scenario. So I go to the driver's side, get in, and turn the ignition, blasting the heat. The windows fog over, and we both catch our breath in what feels like a little cocoon.

"I should've waited for you to pull the truck up," she says, her teeth chattering.

I reach in the back seat for my jacket. The weather up here is so much more unpredictable than in LA. "Here."

She doesn't fight me, just puts her arms in, and the fabric drowns her body.

God, I love seeing her in my clothes.

"Thanks." She puts her hands in front of the heat registers. "We should probably get going."

I nod. Right.

We both put on our seat belts, and I ease out of the parking lot, trying to dodge as many big puddles as I can. Thank goodness I don't have a sports car.

Most of our conversation consists of complaining about being cold and wet, so I turn all the heating vents in her direction.

"No, you need some too." She moves the one closer to me back my way and a blast of hot air dries out my eyes.

"I'm fine. Where do you want to go? Your house, I assume? Unless my house is a possibility..."

She playfully rolls her eyes. "My house please."

"Sure."

The high school was built farther out of town so there was room to expand in the event the town had an influx of people moving here. I learned that at the board meeting, when they discussed building the new elementary school out here as well. But it leaves all the residents winding down one road to get back to downtown.

Halfway back to town, the rain slows and my windshield wipers only have to be on low for me to see clearly. With the defrost on high, it drowns out my music.

"Oh my god!" Posey says at the moment I notice what's in front of us.

A big pile of trees, mud, and debris has slid down the hill next to the road and blocks both lanes of traffic into town. I park the Bronco and climb out. The rain has all but disappeared now, but Mother Nature already did her damage.

"Get back in the truck!" Posey screams out of her window. "You don't know that more of that hillside isn't going to give way."

"I have to see if anyone is in trouble. Someone could be hurt."

She sighs and exits the truck.

"Get back in the truck," I tell her, but she continues walking toward me.

Of course she does. If I told her to come outside, she'd probably stay in the truck.

I tilt my head in every direction, inspecting the area for a car that might've gotten trapped, but the minute I step on a log, it sinks, and I jump back.

"Gavin!" Posey screams.

I laugh, more from being uncomfortable with mud on my clothes than anything else. I've never seen or had anything to do with a mudslide before.

Posey clings to my arm. "Let's go. We have to get out of here." She looks to the left, where the land rises.

We jog back to the truck, and I stare at the pile again. "You don't think this truck can get over that, do you?"

"Listen to the Alaskan girl, California boy. This truck, although nice, cannot get over that. Plus, it's dangerous to be here. For a guy who wanted me to stay in the truck, you're willing to put my life at risk to drive over a pile of trees?" Her eyebrows rise to her hairline.

"You know what this means then?"

She inhales. "Yes. We're not going home tonight."

I do a U-turn, and we go back the way we came, past the sign for Greywall and Lake Starlight. Unfortunately, the hotels and motels in Sunrise Bay are on the other side of the mudslide, which leaves us picking between the two other towns. Greywall isn't very touristy, so I drive toward Lake Starlight.

"Can you call Glacier Pointe Resort?" I ask.

"We're not staying there. Do you know how much it costs?"

"I'll pay," I tell her, trying to look out for any other mudslides that might happen.

"You're not paying for me. I'm not some woman who needs you to take care of her."

I blow out a breath and stop at a stop sign. "What do you suggest then?"

"It's so typical that you'd have to go to the biggest, most expensive place."

"Typical?" I tilt my head and look at her. "What are you implying?"

She taps on her phone, no doubt looking for anywhere else to spend the night. "Famous. Rich. Always wants all the amenities. We're going to sleep, not do a spa night."

I laugh and press on the gas. Her back falls into the seat of the truck. "And here I was really hoping for a massage and a soak. If I wanted a mud bath, I could've just done that back there."

She doesn't say anything.

"You are aware that you don't know that much about me, right?"

She turns in my direction. Finally, a reaction. "It wasn't an insult. It just shows how different we are."

"Fine. Go ahead. Find us somewhere to stay."

I don't mention that we won't be the only ones looking

for rooms. It's tourist season for both Sunrise Bay and Lake Starlight, which means there won't be a lot of vacancies to begin with. And that's before all the people who live in Sunrise Bay can't get home and need somewhere to stay the night.

But I keep my mouth shut and let her try to take care of it.

She makes a phone call, and the first place says they're booked. We pass a small motel that has their no vacancy sign lit up. I still don't say one word.

She continues calling as I drive through all the outskirts. A half hour later, I pull up at the Glacier Pointe Resort and park in the lot, waiting for her to finish talking to another place that told her they were full.

"I can't believe this." She twists to face me, eyes narrowed.

"What choice do we have?"

"Well, I'm paying for myself," she says and gets out of my truck.

Whatever. Let's just hope they have rooms.

I follow her into the lobby. A lot of people are coming in and out—probably because it's Saturday night. Another problem with finding lodging. Some people only come for weekend getaways. A bad feeling rests in my stomach as we approach the front desk.

A woman greets us.

"Do you have any rooms?" Posey asks. She's clearly in a take-charge mindset right now.

The woman looks us over. I have mud caked up to my knees, our clothes are wrinkled and damp, and our hair is... well, I'm sure Posey wouldn't be handing out her business cards right now. We don't look like we belong in this fancy hotel with expensive chandeliers.

"You stuck here because of that mudslide?" the woman asks. "We've been getting reports from a few guests. Unfortunately, I just sold our last room." She's apologetic and purses her lips as if she's trying to find a solution. "I wish I could give you the name of a place nearby, but the closest hotel I know of that has rooms is in Anchorage because—"

"Tourist season. I know." Posey's forehead thumps on the counter. I put my arm around her shoulders and peel her away from the desk.

"Thank you so much," I say to the woman and guide Posey back to my truck.

Once we're seated, we both stare out the window.

"I should've called here first," she says.

I hold up my hands. "I didn't say anything."

"You were thinking it."

"Don't assume you know what I'm thinking." Although I was thinking it, I'm not the type to throw the fact that I was right in someone's face. "Let's just try to find somewhere else."

Her phone rings and she pulls it out of her bag. "It's my mom," she says softly, swiping her thumb over the screen. "Hey, Mom, how's Hank?"

There's a pause, and I hear Marla saying something.

"Okay. I'm glad." Another pause. "Yeah, we didn't get past it. Really?" She covers the receiver. "Jed just got by the mudslide before it happened. He's home with Emilia."

"That's good," I say.

"We've tried everywhere. Even Glacier Pointe. All booked." She listens for a few seconds. "I'll call you as soon as we find somewhere. Yes, I'm fine. Thanks. Take care of Hank. Love you too." She hangs up and rests her hands with her phone tucked between them in her lap. "This might be where we're staying the night. Unless you want to go all the way to Anchorage."

I start the truck and pull out of the parking lot. "There has to be somewhere." Just then, an idea strikes me. "I have a place in mind."

"Where?" she asks, sounding excited.

"I have connections up here too." I wink and she groans.

Five minutes later, I pull up to Griffin and Phoenix's house, but it's completely dark. There's no sign of life inside the house, but I figure it's worth a try.

"Stay here, I'll be back."

She grabs my arm before I can climb out. "Is this Griffin Thorne and Phoenix Bailey's house?"

"Yeah."

"Holy shit. Of course you're friends with them."

I jog up to the door and ring the doorbell. Nothing. I ring the doorbell again. Nothing.

I send a quick text message to Griffin, and he responds that they're in LA. I'm not about to ask to spend the night here without them, so I tell him to hit me up when he gets back.

Returning to the truck, I shake my head. "No luck."

"My mom just texted me a place," Posey says with zero enthusiasm.

"Where?"

Ten minutes of following her directions later, I pull down a long driveway. Trees line the drive on either side. It's eerie and a little scary if you ask me, but the large building is all lit up once we reach the clearing.

"Northern Lights Retirement Center?" I ask, reading the welcome sign.

"Grandma Ethel lives here. We can stay in her apartment."

I park and we both stare at the entrance. It's really come to this?

"Well, desperate measures, I suppose." I climb out of the truck.

We walk through the sliding doors, and I'm not prepared for what I see. This is a retirement home, right?

Chapter Nineteen

Gavin

"Grandma Ethel!" Posey screeches.

From the reception area, we see numerous elderly people pulling condoms down bananas.

I bust out laughing. "Holy shit. This is where we're gonna stay?"

Posey hits me in the stomach, and I bend forward, pretending she knocked the breath out of me. I'm rewarded with her glare. The one that turns me on.

I have a feeling if she knew it turned me on, she wouldn't do it anymore.

Grandma Ethel stands from her chair, a condom hanging off the tip of the banana in her hand. "Posey, sweetie, what're you doing?"

"I think I need to ask you the same thing," she whispers, meeting her grandma halfway.

"Gavin, so nice to see you again." Grandma Ethel slides past Posey to say hello. She kisses my cheek, meaning I have to bend almost in half to reach her. "You look dirty."

"That's what she said," someone from the other room shouts.

"Get your mind out of the gutter!" Dori yells and joins us in the reception area. "They think we need sex education. There was an outbreak of an STD at a home in Anchorage last month. Not sure what that has to do with us. We sneak into different retirement homes."

I can't stop laughing, biting my lip to force myself not to laugh out loud again. While Posey looks as if she wants to cover her ears and scream to make it all stop.

Posey leans closer to Grandma Ethel. "Can I talk to you in private?"

She straightens up. "You know you can trust Dori."

I guess that's a no.

"There was a mudslide, and we can't get back to Sunrise Bay. We've tried getting a room everywhere and no luck."

"Glacier Pointe? Dori's son-in-law owns—"

"We tried. They were full before we got there," I add.

I get another death glare from Posey as she says, "You're not one to rub it in, huh?"

I hold up my hands. "I was just answering her question. I didn't say, 'Posey didn't want me to pay for her room and she likes to support the little man, so while she called every B and B in the county, Glacier Pointe filled up.'"

She turns to face me, narrowing her eyes. "You're ridiculous. I should make you sleep in your truck."

"This is a big place, surely we can sleep separately. Hell, I'll sleep on the table out here if I have to."

"Okay, settle down. I don't go to your place and start bickering and embarrassing you." Grandma Ethel takes Posey's arm and guides her down the hall.

I follow and look at a bunch of arthritic fingers trying to get condoms down bananas.

"I need a Magnum. I'm not used to working with something so small," one man calls to the instructor.

"Shut up, Isaac," a woman calls back. "Try extra small."

The man raises his cane in the air. "Get some glasses next time."

"I go on how it feels," she says with a huff.

Dori puts her arm through mine and guides me down the hallway. "Can you believe they think we don't know how to use a condom? I only had one son, so suffice it to say I used birth control quite successfully. My son, on the other hand..." She shakes her head. "Nine kids. Maybe I should've had a sit-down with him." She laughs.

"Do you have a place here?" I ask Dori. "Maybe I could stay with you. On the couch, obviously."

She pats my hand. "I'm sorry, but my grandsons wouldn't be comfortable with you staying with me."

"Okay." Did she think I was asking her out or something?

"Ethel, there's that one room." Dori nods in the other direction.

"We'll just stay with you, Grandma Ethel," Posey says. "I can take the couch and Gavin can take the floor." She smiles at me as if she's proving something.

Did she think I would take the couch away from her? She doesn't know me at all.

Posey moves to a door that I assume is Grandma Ethel's place, but Ethel puts herself in front of it. "Sorry, I just had my carpets cleaned."

Posey steps back. "I'll take off my shoes."

"Look at you two. You're filthy. I'm not a rich woman and I don't want to pay for the carpet to get cleaned again. Besides, they have to dry overnight."

Dori keeps nodding at Ethel.

"Then Dori?" Posey swings around to face her.

"I already said my grandsons wouldn't like a man sleeping in my apartment." She points at me as if I'm her stalker or something.

"Then can I stay with you and Gavin can stay with one of the male residents?"

I cringe. Is she going to throw me in with Magnum Isaac? No, thank you.

"Sorry, but Ethel's staying with me," Dori says. "I don't have the room."

Posey throws her hands in the air, tears welling in her eyes. "Seriously? I'm so tired. You're grandmas and you're just letting us go back outside where a wild animal could eat us alive?"

Somewhat dramatic, but it's been a long day, so I get it.

"Oh, sweetie, I just meant you can't stay with us, but we do have a room for you. Sometimes guests are snuck in and don't get out before the doors lock for the night so they can't leave until morning." Grandma Ethel's eyes widen. "The helpers don't know about it, so you'll have to be quiet."

Is this gray-haired old biddy talking about booty calls?

"We'll take anything," Posey says, sounding relieved.

"Let's go then. I have to get the key from Olive," Dori whispers.

We follow Dori back to the cafeteria and she weaves through the tables. She talks to a silver-haired woman who looks around before sliding her hand in her bra and retrieving a key.

"I'm not touching it," I say to Posey.

"Grow up." She elbows me and I hold my side.

"What was that for?"

She frowns. "I don't know. I'm sorry."

God, this woman. I chuckle at the fact that she can't even be that mean to me.

Dori comes back over, but as she reaches us, another woman joins us.

"And you are?" Her name tag says she's Leeann.

"This is my granddaughter, and you know Gavin Price, right?" Ethel's voice raises an octave. "Hollywood heart-throb, superstar actor."

Leeann stares at me as if she's trying to place me but can't.

"Blake Michaels," Posey whispers.

Leeann's eyes pop open. "Oh man, I heard you were moving up here. *High Society*, right? You were such a dick."

"That's what she said," a male voice says behind us. No one laughs.

"My character was, yeah."

"But you were so horrible when you were playing both of those innocent girls." She leans in. "I always liked you with Samantha. You were a good couple. Is it true that you dated in real life?"

Posey makes a sound of displeasure and I glance over to see her roll her eyes.

"We did, but it was short lived."

Posey grunts again.

"Why don't you two sit in with us? I'm sure they'd rather hear the stories from the famous actor rather than me drone on about condoms. Even though you can't get pregnant, there's still a need for safe sex." She says the last sentence louder as if it's for the residents' benefit.

"I'm tired," Posey says, then she flings her arm forward. "Ouch." She holds her upper arm and looks back at Ethel.

"They'd love to," Ethel says.

Leeann claps and turns to go back where she was.

"She can't find out you're staying here because no one can find out we have the key to the room," Ethel whispers.

"I'm tired," Posey whines.

"Suck it up, buttercup," Dori says and lightly shoves me forward. "Go win the crowd over."

I look back, but Leeann pats a stool next to her. What warped world am I living in right now?

Posey exaggerates her motions, pulling out a chair and flopping into it.

"This is Gavin Price from the television shows *The Carters* and *High Society*. I think you've done some films too, right?"

"Nothing that did great," I mumble. I had some B movies at best. Other than that, I did some teenage movies that will never see the light of day.

One of the men raises his hand. "How much ass you get?"

"Okay, Miles, we're not going to ask Gavin sexual questions," Leeann says with censure in her voice.

"Then what's the point?" He waves her off and shakes his head.

I laugh. "Honestly, it's probably not what you think."

"But you're all good-looking people," a woman says.

"We also all have our problems. Some aren't happy in the industry. Some feel pressured to do certain things to propel their careers. Some are pissed they're getting passed up. Everyone is kind of lost in their own heads. And relationships?" I huff. "How can you have one when you're on opposite sides of the country most of the time, and even if you're not, you're on set for sixteen hours a day?"

"Hookups on set then?" the same man asks. "What about a sex scene? I'm sure your sausage popped up."

I glance at Posey, who's no longer grumpy but looks as if she's enjoying watching me in the hot seat. "I didn't get a hard-on because I didn't like my costars. It really is acting. Trust me when I say there's nothing sexy about filming a sex scene."

"I don't buy it. I'd be all over their asses," a balding man says.

"Shut up, Al. You know as well as I do that you struggle to get it up, even with the blue pills," another woman says.

"Not when I was his age. Hell, why is he here on a Saturday night? I'd be out chasing tail."

"Why don't we ask Gavin about the acting process?" Leeann places her hand on my knee, and I stiffen a bit. "And they wonder why I have to give them a sex talk."

I laugh and my gaze veers to Posey, who doesn't look happy again.

"Because that's boring." The man who spoke uses his cane to get up. He flips me a condom. "Put that to good use and come back and tell me the story."

I catch the condom, shaking my head.

"Where are you going, Isaac?" Leeann asks.

"If you must know, Leeann, I'm going to watch porn and pleasure myself. Aren't you glad you asked?"

I raise my eyebrows at Leeann, and she smacks on the fakest smile.

"Rowdy bunch here?" I ask.

"You can say that again," she murmurs. "Is everyone done for the night?"

People start to stand and leave, retiring to their rooms.

"I'm a really big fan, Gavin. I could probably ask you a million questions, but I have to clean this up and make sure everyone is settled in before I can relax for the night. Are you staying in Lake Starlight?"

I shift in place. Leeann is cute. She's got that girl next door vibe like Posey, which is my go-to type. But I glance over my shoulder at Posey, who's quietly arguing with Ethel over something that she'll probably lose, and I know where my heart is. "No, Sunrise Bay."

"Oh, our enemy. I actually live in Greywall, but if you're ever bored and want me to show you what Alaska has to offer, give me a call." She scribbles her phone number on the back of a safe sex pamphlet and hands it to me.

I put it in my pocket and smile, not wanting to make her feel bad that I have zero interest in calling her. "Nice to meet you."

"You too."

"Gavin!" Dori shouts as if she's my grandma and I just stole a pack of gum at the supermarket.

I walk away from Leeann, back to the three of them. "What?"

"We have limited time to get you in there."

"Man, you *are* gifted. Picking up women at retirement homes too?" Posey crosses her arms.

"Jealous?" I hope like hell she is.

"Never." She stomps forward, following Grandma Ethel through the building.

We turn down a corridor and around one more corner. Where the hell are they taking us?

While Dori is the lookout, Ethel uses the key to open a room at the end of the hall. Once the door opens, Ethel pulls us inside. Dori follows and lightly shuts the door, looking the entire time to make sure no one sees us.

They turn on the light and Posey looks up at me at the exact time I look down at her.

One bed. The dynamic duo strikes again. Figures.

Posey

"No way." I walk closer to Grandma Ethel, but there's not enough room in here for me to get her alone. "I know you probably want to fix us up, but seriously, the whole one bed thing? Come on."

Her eyebrows crinkle. "One bed thing? I'm sorry, I just... you need a place and..."

I've never known Grandma Ethel to be at a loss for words.

"You mean you're not planning some fix up between us?" I give her my most ardent stare.

She puts her hand on mine and squeezes. "I never want to pressure my grandchildren. A nudge here or there is fine, but I wouldn't lock you in a room with one bed to get what I want." She shakes her head like how could I even think that? "I also know you're adults and there's no reason why you can't share a bed platonically. You're both strong-willed individuals and won't let your libidos win, right?"

"Of course not," I rush out, mortified that in a roundabout way, I'm talking to my grandma about sex. "I'm sorry. I just thought..."

She squeezes my hand again and opens her mouth, but there's a knock on the door. Dori opens it a bit, then waves Midge in.

"This is all I've got." Midge hands over a stack of clothes to Dori. "The pajamas are from my late husband, but he didn't die in them or anything. And then I gave you one of my nightgowns. Please return them without stains."

I cough and Gavin's looking at me like seriously, are these women for real?

"Thank you, Midge. Very nice of you." Dori goes to hand them to Gavin, but he doesn't take them, so she places them on the bed. "Once you shower, leave those clothes outside and we'll get them washed for you." She looks at Gavin. "Wait until you see what an iron can do." She looks at the other two women. "This generation never wants to iron anything."

Gavin opens his mouth but closes it, probably figuring it's better if he keeps quiet.

"Thanks, ladies," I say. "We appreciate everything."

I elbow Gavin and he jumps. "Yeah, thanks for your help."

Grandma Ethel places one palm on my cheek and the other on Gavin's. "That's what grandmas are for. You're happy, we're happy." She pats our cheeks. "Don't forget to leave the dirty clothes outside. You have half an hour before Earl will be by to pick them up."

This place runs like a well-oiled underground operation. It's scary that the administrators think they're in charge. This group of seniors could run the world.

Finally they leave, and I shut the door and flick the lock behind them.

"I've been in some sketchy situations in my life—and feel free to take my man card from me—but I'm not sure about staying here."

I laugh and pick up the nightgown so I can head to the

bathroom, needing to get showered and to bed. "What are you afraid of?"

"I'm not sure where to start."

I chuckle. "It's my grandma, we're fine."

He looks around. "This feels like a bomb shelter or something."

"Let's just get showered, leave our clothes for them, and go to bed."

"About that... I'm not wearing a dead man's clothes." He stares at the stereotypical plaid button-up shirt and pajama pants resting on the edge of the bed.

I wave off his concern. "She said he didn't die in them. It's fine."

His jaw hangs ajar. "Come on, Posey, I'm sleeping in my boxer briefs."

"No, you're not! If we're sharing that bed"—I motion with my hand up and down his body—"that has to be covered up."

He walks toward me with that devilish smirk that says he's going to be flirtatious, probably insisting that I don't want him half naked because I want him. And as tired as I am right now, I'd probably admit that that's exactly the reason.

Thankfully, he stubs his toe on his way over to me. "Fuck." He flops down onto the corner of the bed, and because it's a soft mattress, it doesn't support his weight, so he falls to the floor.

I laugh like he did when we first walked into the retirement center. "I'm taking a shower, Rico Suave."

I head into the bathroom and shut the door, wishing I had the nerve to ask Gavin to join me. It's getting harder and harder to remember why he's off-limits and why the two of us together is a recipe for disappointment.

The bathroom is clean but dim. Gavin was right with the whole bomb shelter vibe this place gives off. Inside the shower there's a small shampoo, conditioner, and soap, and I find fresh towels in a cabinet.

I hurry and take a shower. The warm water running down my neck and shoulders feels like heaven. At some point while I'm soaping my body, the thought that I'll be sharing a bed with Gavin floats into my consciousness. Do I have the willpower Grandma Ethel thinks I have? I'm not sure.

Once I'm done, I dry off and take my first good look at the nightgown. Holding it up in the dim light, I feel my eyes bulge. I cannot wear this in front of Gavin. It's formfitting, very lacy, and something meant for seduction.

What is it with these women? Do they have pseudo-lingerie at the ready, just in case?

I slip the silk over my head. It fits like a dream. Obviously Midge hasn't worn this in a while, though I'm starting to doubt it was ever actually hers.

There's a deep V in the center of my breasts and thin straps drape the gorgeous garment off my shoulders. I pick up the long silk skirt with two fingers and pull it away from my legs, twirling around like a princess. The soft pink color pulls out the red in my hair. Now I just have to get from the door into bed without him seeing me.

I open the door a slit. "Turn around."

He's on the edge of the bed, his phone in his hands. "Why? She gave you pajamas. I promise not to jump you while you're in grandma pajamas." He glances over and I slam the door shut.

"I'm serious. Turn around."

He groans. "Fine, but hurry. I just wanna take a shower."

"The sooner you turn away, the sooner you're in the shower."

"Just come out. I won't look."

I peek through the opening to see that his back is to me, so I sprint across the small room and dive under the covers on the bed. "Okay, all clear."

He looks over at me. "Are blankets up to your neck really necessary?"

"If you saw what I'm wearing, you'd understand."

He grabs the blankets at the bottom of the bed. "Maybe I need to check out the view."

I grip the blankets with my fingers until my knuckles are white. "Don't you dare."

He laughs and walks into the bathroom, shutting the door.

I pull the blankets off me a bit and lie in the bed. I actually like this nightie. It's the old-school kind that makes me feel sexy without showing off my ass or nipples. Now most men want a woman naked or half naked, ready and willing. The men I've been with have no appreciation for lingerie or foreplay.

I collect my clothes and knock on the bathroom door. "I need your clothes."

"They're on the floor. I'm in the shower."

"Well, get out and toss them out the door."

"Just come in and get them, I'm not shy."

I growl and inch the door open. "Do not even think about opening that curtain," I warn.

He pretends to ruffle it and I grab his clothes and slam the door. His laugh floats from the other side. Sometimes he makes it hard not to hate him.

I set the clothes outside the door, lock it, and climb back

under the blankets. There is literally nothing to put a barrier between us, so I inch as far as I can on the right side.

It's hard not to think of him naked on the other side of that door. I imagine what he might be doing at that exact moment. Washing his hair, rinsing the suds, running the same soap I used all over his body...

When the water shuts off, my heartbeat accelerates, and I try to calm myself down.

You totally have this, Posey. You're going to be fine. He's just going to sleep beside you. It's no different than if he was Mandi.

I close my eyes as he opens the door.

"I know you're not asleep. I heard your grunts of frustration."

I open my eyes and shut them again. "You're only wearing a towel!"

"That's because you took my boxer briefs and I already told you I'm not wearing a dead man's pajamas."

I sit up to fight with him and the sheet falls to my lap, but I recover quickly before he catches a glimpse. "You're not sleeping in this bed naked."

"I'll leave the towel on," he says, but the wicked smirk says he's playing with me.

I shake my head vigorously. "No way."

He puts his arms out to his sides. "I don't know what you want me to do. You took my boxer briefs."

"Because you have pajamas."

"Again, a dead man's pajamas."

I growl and flop back onto the mattress, kicking and screaming like a child.

"You're going to alert someone to us being in here," he says.

I roll over on my side. "Fine. Turn off the lights. Whatever. I just need to sleep, but if you try to spoon me at some point, I can't be blamed for what happens."

"That's the kind of threat that makes Erwin scared of you." He turns off the lights and the mattress dips.

I inhale and exhale, trying to remain calm and steady my breathing, but my body thinks it's about to have a big chocolate cake all to itself and doesn't cooperate. "I'm not scary."

"To Erwin you are. Not to me. I actually enjoy your numerous moods."

I move to roll over but stop myself. "I do not have mood swings."

"I didn't say you did. I said numerous moods, but let's go to bed. You're cranky when you don't sleep."

I guffaw. "Okay, you have no way of knowing that."

"Sorry, I assumed. I guess I'm an ass."

"Yes, you are," I say and dramatically throw myself into the mattress. "Good night." I tug the covers tighter to me.

"Good night," he says, sweet and soft.

Silence falls over the dark room. The last thing I'm going to do tonight is sleep. I can't see him at all, but I can *feel* that he's close. It's like my body is plugged into a generator and energy thrums through my veins.

"You know I run into people like Leeann all the time." His voice is low.

"What?"

"People who only see me for what I've done. Don't you wonder why Leeann would give me her number when she doesn't even know me? I know you saw, and I know you're jealous."

I huff. "I'm not jealous."

"Good."

I exhale and take the bait. "Why is that good?"

"Because if we're going to be together, then you'll have to learn to deal with women fawning over me."

I snort. "You really do think highly of yourself."

"Not really. It's the opposite mostly."

There's a pang in my chest. "How could that be?"

He moves around as though he can't get comfortable. "You know how many shitty things I've read about myself? That my acting sucks. How it's too bad I couldn't have stayed eight years old. They don't like my haircut, what was I thinking about when I wore that. Everything down to did I put on a few extra pounds to I have small feet and you know what that means. It's all such bullshit."

I can't say I haven't seen the gossip, even if I don't actively seek it out, and for the first time, I feel guilty about it. I roll over, keeping the sheet tight against me. "I can't imagine that's easy to deal with."

"Do you wanna know why I want to be mayor?"

All I can see is the silhouette of him. I'm not sure I want the answer to the question my mom told me to ask him.

"You don't have to tell me," I say, because his answer might just prove wrong everything I've allowed myself to believe about him.

He shifts his weight to face me. "I just want to help people. I want to put policies in place that help those less fortunate. I want to have a community where people feel safe and secure and like they're a part of something."

"Why Sunrise Bay?" I ask.

He clicks his tongue off the roof of his mouth. "That's easy. The minute I step over the city limit, I feel like I've been transported somewhere else. Like the outside world doesn't matter and almost like..."

"What?"

"It's stupid."

"Tell me."

There's still a long pause. "I want to help preserve what you have here. I want to protect it, the people, you."

"From what?"

"I told you it's stupid. Let's talk about something else."

"Gavin," I say, my voice hopefully transparent enough that he knows he can trust me with this.

"I want to protect you from the ugliness of the world."

And there it is. Maybe he does love this town as much as I do. And of course, with that, my heart floats right out of my chest and into his hands for him to do what he will with it.

Posey

"If you tell anyone that, I might have to start a rumor that you did permanent damage when you cut my ear," he whispers.

"I promise, it's safe with me. But I'm going to be honest, you would've won my vote with that reason. That's what you should be telling people when you campaign." I can't believe I just confessed that, but it's the truth. Still, I feel like a traitor to my mom.

My eyes have adjusted to the darkness of the room, and since we're facing one another now, I can make out his face.

He smiles. "That's the nicest thing you've ever said to me."

"If only you weren't competing against my mom. Who knows what could've happened?"

He stares at me for a long moment, and I squirm under his attention. "I think about it all the time."

"Gavin..." I turn my face away from his.

He reaches under my chin and urges me to look at him. "Don't shy away from me. You're beautiful."

"You can't say things like that. I have to hate you."

He chuckles softly. "I don't believe you hate me, but it does make me all hot when you pretend to."

I push him in the shoulder. "I'm fully aware what you

must be thinking about me wanting my mom to win so bad."

"Don't go thinking you know what's going on in my head. I might be wondering what exactly they're doing with our clothes right now."

A laugh bubbles out of me. It feels really good after the night we've had.

"In all seriousness, I saw my mom at her lowest. I'm not sure kids are supposed to see their parents like that. Not at the age of eight anyway. I mean, maybe when they're older and they need your assistance, like Grandma Ethel."

Gavin chuckles. "I'm not sure anyone in this building needs any assistance from their children."

"True enough."

"Continue though," he says softly.

"She had nothing after she split from my dad. We moved to Sunrise Bay, lived with my grandparents. She was so depressed." I shrug. "Maybe when we were in Arizona, it was all an act, but she would be up and showered before us, make us breakfast, have our lunches all in order. My dad came home some nights at dinnertime, and he would kiss her hello, whisper something in her ear that made her smile. He'd check in with our homework, talk to Jed about whatever sport he was playing." I sigh. "It really felt like we were straight out of a sitcom. Like we were the Carters."

He huffs. "The Carters were fictional, Posey. We weren't a real family."

"I know, but—"

He takes my hand, holding it between us. "I understand. Hell, I was on the show and wished it was my real family. Even with my actor dad snorting coke during breaks and my actor mom screwing my fictional brother in the dressing room."

My mouth opens. "Seriously?"

"Uh-huh." He nods.

"Damn."

"Yeah. But I keep interrupting you. Please finish."

"It's not really an original story. After the affair came out, she said we were moving. Jed blew up. Dad said she couldn't take him, that Jed needed to be with his dad if he was ever going to go Dɪ, but Mom told him she'd take him for everything if he tried to take Jed from her. They made some arrangement and whatever it was, it left her with nothing but child support. She'd never worked a day in her life, and she struggled to pick herself back up."

"But clearly she did. She's an amazing woman."

I nod, tears welling when I think of how far she's come. "She is. Hank helped her see her true self. The one who was there before my dad ruined her. But I was the one who'd stay with her at night and watch movies. I tried to make new traditions and new memories to fill the void of what she lost. Because although I didn't know it then, you lose everything with divorce. It's not just the parents, it's all the family traditions. The little things that you did all your life. Soon, you're not coloring eggs the night before Easter because you have to spend it with your dad. I didn't have it half as bad as Jed, since my dad didn't really want much to do with me."

He squeezes my hand and frowns. "I'm sorry."

"Yeah, well, I've seen Jed's side too and I'm not sure it's much better to be his prized pet, either. Dad did a number on him for sure."

"It's amazing how much childhood bullshit can screw you up. Twist your beliefs and how you see things." He rolls onto his back.

We lie in silence for a few minutes, listening to the steady hum of our breathing.

After a while, he rolls back over to face me. "I'm gonna lay it out there, Posey. I really like you and I wish I could take myself off that ballot, but I've done what other people wanted me to my entire life. What my parents or my agent thought was best. But rehab taught me that if I'm really going to stay sober, I need to run my own life. I need to set goals and accomplish them. I need to do the things that light me up inside. But you have no idea what a weakness you are to that newfound strength of mine. How much I want to say fuck the campaign and take you out again."

My breath lodges in my throat. "Gavin…" I'm unsure how to respond. "I'd never expect you to give up on your goal. Is that what you think? That I want you to give up what makes you happy? Never." I sit up and lean on the wall, since the bed has no headboard. "I think we're just stuck in a situation that doesn't have an easy answer."

"Stuck because you want me too?" There's so much hope in his voice.

He's so forthcoming with his desires that it demands I be too. I bite my lip and nod.

"Yeah," I say softly, finally admitting my feelings to him.

He sighs, and it sounds pained rather than relieved. "I can separate the election from us, but I see why you can't." He inches closer, resting his head in his palm.

I look down to see his gaze on me. I forgot to pull the blanket up when I sat up against the wall and the snug silk pulls across my breasts, the lace V teasing the crevice of them.

My breathing hitches in my throat and an ache forms in my center. "I can't. But you have no idea how tempting you are right now. How badly I want to throw off these covers and say to hell with it." I bury my face in my hands.

The mattress shifts, and he sits up, pulling my hands

away from my face. "It could be our secret. Until after the campaign, obviously."

I glance at his bare chest and press my teeth into my bottom lip. He's harder than ever to deny.

"Seeing you in this... it's hard to control myself. All I want to do is touch you, kiss you, fuck you." The softness of his voice surrounds me like a thick blanket.

I want everything he said too. I've wanted it since our first date.

"But I won't make a move unless you tell me it's okay." He stares at me with intensity that I can *feel*.

I trail my fingertips over his lips, then down his body until they're bouncing off every ab and they rest on the sheets and blankets that conceal him from me. "Are you really naked?"

He nods.

My mind conjures up what he might look like. How big he might be, how his hands will feel on me, how he'll feel inside me.

I love my mom and I want her to be happy, but I need to take this one for me and reap the repercussions tomorrow. Otherwise, I'll always wonder.

I smash my lips to his and he wraps his arms around my waist, pulling me down on him. He's all hard body to my soft curves and his tongue doesn't wait for permission, just plunges into my mouth and claims me. He makes me feel wanton, as though he's been waiting an eternity to taste me and now that he has, it'll never be enough.

"Goddamn." He rolls me over and rises up on his hands to take me beneath him. "You're so beautiful and this... I feel like I'm taking away your innocence."

I laugh. "I'm not a virgin."

His finger runs the length of the V, dipping under the

lace and teasing my breast. "Thank God, because I'm not sure I have the willpower to fuck you like I'd have to if you were a virgin."

A five-alarm fire engulfs my body. His words, his actions, the look on his face, all work together to make him irresistible. I wrap one arm around his neck and pull him down. Again, our lips collide and our tongues tangle in a fury.

He nudges my legs apart with his knees and the silk nightgown slides up my legs. With the help of his hands and me raising my ass, he gets the fabric to rest at my waist, then I feel his length at my core.

"God, you feel so good," I whisper.

He places his hands on my face, resting his elbows on either side of my head, and kisses me slowly and passionately. "This isn't a one-time thing for me, Posey, I want you to know that."

I groan when he circles his hips. I widen my legs, wanting him so badly, but he slides one strap of my nightgown off my shoulder.

"I'm torn. I want to fuck you so bad with this on, but I want to see you bared to me more." I help him slide one arm out, and he pulls the fabric down to reveal my breast. "Perfection."

My back arches when he places his mouth over my breast, twirling my nipple with his tongue. As he takes his time devouring one breast, his fingers travel up my rib cage, slipping the other strap off my shoulder.

He draws back, taking me in, and I'm not embarrassed as I have been with other men. I have a confidence with Gavin that I never knew was inside me.

He presses my breasts together and switches the nipple he's sucking, then lets go with a pop. "I'm going to fuck these one day."

I sigh, unable to take much more anticipation. He travels down my stomach, his gaze never straying from mine for long. I help him get the nightgown off me, and he situates himself between my legs, using his fingers to spread me open.

"You're dripping," he says, plunging one finger inside before his mouth touches my clit.

I moan and my ass rises off the bed. He adds another finger and arches them.

"Please. Please," I beg mindlessly, needing him inside me.

Instead of moving his fingers, he holds them there while his tongue flicks my clit. I writhe under him, needing more movement of his fingers, but he's playing a game with me. A game that's taking me to the edge and not letting me fall over.

"I need you, Gavin. Please don't make me wait any longer." My hands entwine through his silky hair.

"Just one or two more minutes." He winks and licks me before sucking my clit into his mouth.

He moves his fingers now, and I lose myself in the pleasure he's giving me, his fingers and mouth working in a perfect rhythm. I cry out with the orgasm my body has been begging for since I first met Gavin Price. He chuckles into my core, pressing the softest kiss to my pussy before rising up on the bed. He situates himself on top of me but rolls me over with him so I'm on top.

"Too tired to take the reins?" I ask.

He caresses my cheek. "Just greedy. I want to watch your tits move and see how your second orgasm flushes your beautiful porcelain skin."

My fingers run down his chest. "Condom?"

His eyes widen. "Shit. I had one in the pocket of my pants from the meeting."

My stomach sinks. No, no, no.

He gently moves me off his lap and onto the mattress. "There's got to be one here." He bends over and opens the one drawer in the small bedside table, then pulls out an economy-size box of condoms. "I'm scared, Posey. What kind of place is this?"

I laugh, taking the condom from his hand and tearing it open. "Do you really want to worry about that now?" I pinch the tip of the condom and roll it down his length. "And for the record—apparently small feet have no bearing on dick size."

He chuckles and relaxes back, one hand reaching up and squeezing my breast. "Ride me, baby," he says in a seductive voice that makes me burn for him.

I situate myself over him, guiding his cock inside me. His hands mold to my hips and I fall forward, kissing him because he's the most mouthwatering man I've ever seen and I can't believe he's inside me right now.

"Posey, I need you to move," he says in a strained voice.

I giggle, circling my hips. I sit up straighter, leaning back a bit and resting my hands on his thighs, and rock in a circle that leaves a smoldering gaze in his eyes.

"Damn, this better not be my dream and I wake up before I finish."

"No dream," I say.

But all the teasing and talk has made us both more than eager, so our movements go from teasing to frantic as the tension builds. We're trying to be quiet, but at the same time, we're telling each other how good it is with loud whispers.

His hands explore every part of my body he can reach, leaving a tingling sensation in their wake.

"I'm so close," I say and his hand falls between my legs, massaging my clit. Thank goodness for him, but I move his hand away, grinding on his pelvic bone to get the friction I need.

"Take whatever you need from me to get there. I just want to watch you come." He pinches the hard points of my nipples and I moan.

The pleasure increases at a speed I'm not prepared for, leaving me no time to attempt to hold back my orgasm. My body convulses forward with a jolt when my climax hits me, and I cry out. I catch his expression as I'm coming out of my blissful daze. Gavin really is going to get off just by watching me come, using his body as a fuck toy.

I sit up straight, and he pops me off and back down on his dick with a firm grasp on my hips. It feels amazing, and I clench to give him the snuggest feeling I can.

"Shit. Shit. Posey," he says as he raises his hips and stills inside me, his fingernails digging into my hip bones. After a few pumps of his steel length, he collapses back down to the mattress. "Fuck, you're amazing."

I rest my head on his chest and he moves my sweaty hair away from my face.

"I'm going to have to be careful. You could be my next addiction."

Bringing my chin to his chest, I look up at him. "You say the sweetest things."

His body vibrates with laughter. "It was meant in the best way possible. I promise."

I kiss his chest. "I know."

Our gazes lock for a moment, and there's so much

emotion between us that I could drown in it. If we don't make it, I'm walking away broken for sure.

Chapter Twenty-two

Gavin

I'm not sure what time it is when I stir, but the moment I do, I'm blowing red hair away from my mouth. Posey moves her naked body away from mine, but I hook an arm around her to keep her in place. "You're not getting away that fast."

"You're not done after last night?" she asks in a groggy voice I'd love to wake up to every morning.

"Hell no. I'll never tire of you," I say, kissing the top of her head.

She slides over me and pulls the blanket away. "I had this whole idea of waking you up with my mouth."

I run my hand along her hairline, moving her hair out of the way so I can see her. She licks up my length, teasing the tip with her tongue before she covers my entire head with her warm mouth.

"Fuck." I learned last night how good she is at this, but I didn't let her finish me off because all I wanted was to be buried deep inside her.

She moans and I grow harder in her mouth.

"I'm not gonna last long," I say through staggered breaths.

She looks up at me with a flirtatious glance, like she's going to treat it like a challenge. She pulls me inside her mouth with one long, deep pull and I stare at the ceiling to gather myself. With dragged-out movements, she teases me, taking me to the edge I won't come back from. I raise my ass off the bed, thrusting into her mouth and enticing a sound from her that makes me want to spill down her throat.

She takes everything I give her, even adding her hand to the base to pump me. After that, it doesn't take long before I'm fucking her mouth, taking charge, eager to get to the finish line.

"Shit, baby, I'm coming."

She doesn't move, and I growl as cum rushes up my cock. I pump into her, and she swallows me down, then licks me clean.

"You're utter perfection and I am undeserving of you."

She smiles. "Finally, you realize what everyone else already knows." Then she falls onto her back, laughing.

She sits up, still naked, and I love that she's not insecure and doesn't try to cover up. My fingers graze down the side of her body.

"Are you sure this wasn't a mistake?" she asks, worry filling her eyes.

"Hell no." I sit up and get her back on the mattress, falling on top of her. "I know there're some things we'll have to sort out, but we will. Let's just enjoy this."

"But we'll keep it quiet, right?"

I sigh because I don't want to keep it quiet, but I understand the situation she's in with her mom. "If that's what you want, but I'm only giving you until after the election."

"Deal." She inches forward and kisses my chin. "I think we should get dressed."

"Spend the night at my place tonight." I'm just shy of begging.

With her hand on my chest, she pushes, but I don't move. "We have to be careful."

A knock sounds on the door and I practically jump off the bed.

Posey grabs the nightgown and slips it on. I had her put it back on last night just so I could fuck her in it. I'm definitely going to be on the search for vintage nightgowns.

She inches the door open a crack. "Oh, thank you. Yep, we'll be right down."

Whoever it is tries to look in, but Posey shuts the door. She holds up our clothes that are now hanging in plastic as though they came from the dry cleaners.

"You find it weird that Earl might have been the one to fold your panties?" I ask.

"Ew." She shoves me. "Don't say that."

I climb out of bed and get dressed. "I think they pressed these." I hold up my black boxers that are pinned to a wire hanger.

She laughs and puts on her panties. Damn, I can't wait to slip those off her body, to tease her over the thin silk. Although last night was amazing, there's so much more I can't wait to experience with her.

Once we're both dressed, we make the bed, but I'm really hoping someone comes in and washes these sheets.

"What do we do with these?" I hold up the dead man's pajamas and the nightgown.

Posey picks up the nightgown. "I think I fell in love with this." She sighs and sets it down. "I guess we should just leave them here. It's too suspicious if we bring them down to breakfast."

She's right, so we leave them on the edge of the bed and walk out of the room. You can hear a game of Bingo going on in the cafeteria, so we follow the sounds of the voices. I hold her hand, but as soon as we hit the hall of the cafeteria, she releases my hold with a smile. We did agree, so I can't complain.

"Posey!" Grandma Ethel exclaims, standing. "You came by this morning." She looks toward the aide sitting at a table off the side.

Posey doesn't miss a beat. "Yeah, well, I was in Lake Starlight, so we wanted to say goodbye."

"Stay. There's plenty of food, and some of us have questions after Gavin's Q and A last night." She looks at the aide. "Leeann surprised us after the safe sex talk that we really needed to hear."

Shit, they're like kids who are well-behaved in front of their parents but holy terrors away from them.

Posey looks at me, and I shrug.

"Okay," she says.

Ethel leads us over to grab our breakfast. We both make a plate and, on my way back to the table, a few people wink at me, giving me the eye like they know I had sex last night.

I'm completely weirded out by this place. I can't get out of here fast enough.

Ethel, Dori, and Midge join us. As do Earl and Isaac, the cane guy from last night.

Midge leans over, looking around to make sure no one is listening. "Did you like the nightgown?"

Posey's face lights up. "I did. It's so beautiful."

"I know. I hope you have the same luck in it that I did." She looks dreamy now, as though she's left our table and traveled back in time to when she wore it.

"Oh, um... no. We didn't." Posey looks at me and I'm sure her blush is more telling than her adamant tone.

"No, we did not," I confirm.

Ethel's eyebrows raise.

"I heard you, I'm right on the other side of that room," Isaac says. Posey nearly chokes on her eggs, and he waves her off. "It's fine. What happens here stays here. We don't gossip about who sleeps with who."

"Like Vegas," Earl says.

I sigh and stare down at my plate.

"Well then, I guess you know our secret." Posey sounds less than thrilled.

"I think it's great." Ethel beams at me. "Posey's always been so stubborn, but you've persevered. That says a lot. I knew when your meet-cute was you running her off the road that it was a match." She acts as if I just proposed to Posey.

"Nothing says romance like dangerous driving and potential vehicular manslaughter," Posey deadpans.

"Could you imagine if it still has the same effect all these years later?" Midge interrupts, still in some other universe.

"Eat so we can leave," Posey murmurs.

"You seem like you were a generous lover," Isaac says to me.

A small whimper leaves Posey, and I pile a forkful of eggs into my mouth.

"So, you'll tell me, won't you?" Midge pats Posey's hand.

She swallows her bacon and looks at Midge's hopeful expression. "Tell you what?"

"If you're with child. I conceived all my children in that nightgown. We had some wonderful nights."

I choke and cough all my eggs onto my plate.

Another whimper comes from Posey, a little louder this time.

"I really think we need to go. I have to get back to the campaign place and... let's just go, Posey." I'm done being polite, as I pick up her tray and walk them back to the kitchen.

While I'm away from everyone, I inhale and exhale. What if that nightgown has some weird type of magic juju? Hell, I want to date Posey, but I'm not ready to have a kid yet.

"You look like you saw a ghost," Posey says, coming up behind me and laughing.

"Did you hear her?"

"Yep." She puts her hands on her stomach, rubbing it as if there could be a baby in there. "You said you were all in. Does this change things?" She tilts her head.

Since this whole room knows anyway, I break the distance between us, covering her hand with mine. "Changes nothing. I'd love nothing more than to raise a dozen with you, darling."

"Bullshit," she says and shivers. "Can you believe that? What if it, like, wore off on me or something? I have to shower."

I link her fingers with mine. "Come on. I'm taking you home."

We walk back out and say our goodbyes.

"Thank you for having us," I say, shaking hands with everyone. When I get to Midge, I freeze and stare at her.

Posey bumps into my back and veers around me. I shoot her a look and she laughs again because Midge is playing with a Rubik's Cube.

How do I tell Erwin he needs to come to Northern Lights Retirement Center to get it back?

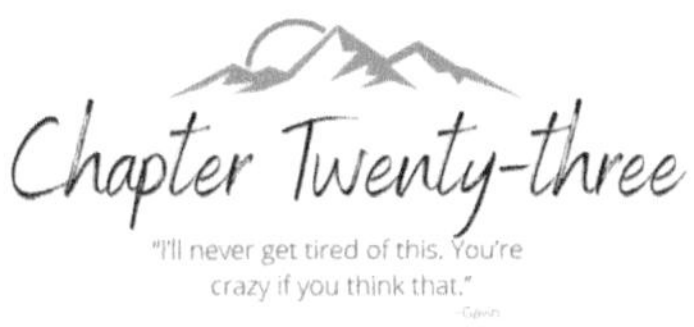

Chapter Twenty-three

Posey

For the past week, I haven't heard one peep about Gavin and me and our hookup at Northern Lights Retirement Center. On the flip side, I've been so paranoid that every time I'm around Gavin, I ignore him, which is going to cause more interest than our usual bickering.

Now, it's Friday and the bell of my door rings at Fringe. I'm cleaning up from my last haircut. Malia left early to do some errands, but the town is bustling, and I thought that since I've been gone so much for my mom, I might get some walk-ins if I stuck around. I just wasn't expecting my walk-ins to start with Gavin.

"You can't be here," I say, resting the broom on the wall by my mirror and walking toward him.

He runs his fingers through his hair. It's been three weeks since the last time I cut it. "I'm here for my haircut. You lost that bet, remember?" He says it loudly, as if he assumes someone's in the back.

"It's only us."

With that knowledge, his gaze slowly peruses my body. I'm wearing a dress with sandals. He hums a hungry sound that unravels the desire inside me.

"That's not an invitation."

"I've gone six days. That has to be a record when we only had one night together." He walks closer, and all I can do is look out the window to make sure no one sees him stalking toward me.

"And we agreed to keep this quiet, remember?" I turn on my heel and walk to the shampoo station, needing to keep this business even if my stomach flutters with excitement.

"As of right now, we're not keeping anything quiet because nothing is happening."

He sits in the chair and slides his hand up my leg as I situate a towel under his neck. I've always been hyperaware of how erotic it can be to wash a man's hair in one of these chairs. My breasts can brush their face, the closeness means I can smell their cologne. I've always been conscious about my movements with any other man, but I want Gavin as bad as he wants me.

"This is your favorite part, remember?" I spray the warm water over his scalp.

"It was my favorite part until I had you under my tongue."

"Damn you and your mouth."

His eyes pop open—they're filled with a hunger that makes my center throb. "Do you not like it when I talk to you like that?"

I scrub his scalp and his eyes slowly drift closed. "The opposite actually."

His finger trails up my leg, but he's not at the best vantage point. Still, an audible moan escapes me, wishing he could bring it up farther between my legs.

"I really want to feel your panties. Will you let me?"

I rinse his hair and ignore his question.

But once I'm finished and drying his hair with a towel before having him sit up straight, he swings his arm around my waist to pull me down onto him. "Well, what do you think?"

I push off his chest. "I think you want us to be on *Scandals of Sunrise Bay*. That's what I think."

"Don't you have blinds? What about your office?"

"I'm still open and you're here for a haircut, remember?" I lead him over to my chair.

The only privacy we have is the half wall that separates me from the waiting area.

"Come on, one touch. Let me feel how wet you are." He leans forward, his hand coming up behind my dress.

I look out the window and don't see anyone, so I stay in place. His finger glides up my inner thigh and runs over the silk of my panties, where I was already soaked even before his stroking.

He groans. "That was probably a bad idea." I turn around with a comb and scissors to see him adjusting himself. "But I don't regret it. What color?"

I situate myself behind him, combing his wet hair. "My panties?"

He nods.

I lean in close to his ear and meet his gaze in the mirror. "Red."

He pushes up out of the chair. "Sorry, we need to clear this up right now."

I direct him back down into the chair. "Just hold on and let me cut your hair. Remember the other time you distracted me when I had scissors in my hand?"

He chuckles. "Not so sure that was an accident."

I shake my head, not responding to his accusation. "How is the election? What did you do about Erwin and the Rubik's Cube?"

He appears defeated. "I'd rather debate with you for five

hours than talk to him about it. I don't want to rat Midge out. I mean... it could be hers." I eye him through the mirror, and he lets out a big exhale. "Yeah, I know. He walks around so depressed; I'm just going to buy him one. Even if it won't be his lucky one, maybe it'll do."

I place my hands on his shoulders. "You really like Erwin, don't you?"

He shrugs. "He's different, but he's a good guy."

I cut his hair again. I love having his hair in my fingers and the feel of it makes it hard to concentrate.

"Let's go back to talking about us. I want to take you on a date."

I cough and the scissors almost slip out of my grasp. "Um. No."

"Why not? We can be discreet. Even if I want everyone to know you're mine."

I meet his gaze in the mirror. "Just give me a chance to tell my mom. Besides, the election isn't far away."

He wants to move this along really fast. I'm scared that I might be appealing right now, but once he has me all to himself, he won't want me.

"Then I guess all we have to discuss is your panties and how I want to take them off."

I smack his shoulder. "If you keep this up, I'm going to think you only want me for sex."

He grabs my hips and pulls me onto his lap. Nuzzling his face into my neck, he nibbles on my earlobe. "Baby, I'll fuck you every minute of every day, but if you need me to prove where my loyalty to you is, I will. It's not with my dick, it's with my heart."

His words fill me with both hope and terror. If it's worth having, it's gonna be hard losing.

I'm off his lap as though I was never there to begin with. "You are something."

"You're everything."

I place the scissors and comb down. "Where's the Gavin Price who first came to this town?"

"He's right here. This is Gavin when he wants something."

"And if he doesn't want it after he gets too much of it?" The question leaves my lips in a joking tone, but when I see his face when it soaks in, it's clear I just told him my biggest fear.

The flirtatious vibe rushes out of the salon like a mouse who spotted a cat.

"Is this because I'm an addict or because of your own insecurities?" he asks.

I go back behind him, but our eyes meet in the mirror. He won't let this go.

"A little of both."

He takes off his cape, the snaps making a *pop, pop, pop* sound, and he grabs my hand, tugging me down the hall. Before we get too far, he releases me and walks back over to the door. I hold my breath until he flicks the lock and puts up the closed sign. Then he's back to me, taking my hand and dragging me to the office.

Once we're inside, he picks me up by my waist and places me on the desk. "I want to make something clear, okay?"

I nod.

His hands rest on either side of my hips and he leans forward. "I've been clean for two years. I haven't had a drop, a snort, a pill. Nothing. I'm fully aware that I have an addictive personality. I can never get enough of a good thing. But you have to know something."

He paces in the small space. My stomach sours with the thought of him having another secret to reveal. He has a kid. He has an ex-wife. He's really only here to prepare for a role for a movie set in a small town.

He returns to me, his hands on either side of my hips again, his face right in front of mine. "I've wanted you for a long time, Posey. At the barbecue, I was gonna ask you out, but then I found out I ran you off the road, so I felt like an idiot. That and I wanted to make sure that I was all in here before getting involved with you. You aren't the type of girl I'd ever want just for sex. I like the way we started out. You disliking me. It gave me a chance to get to know you better. You didn't hold anything back."

"But—"

"I'm telling you this because I don't want you to doubt me because you think I'm a sex addict or something. I just want you, that's all. Any way I can get you."

I wrap my arms around his neck and pull him closer. "Then give me time. I don't want my mom to feel betrayed, and I can't help but feel like I'm being disloyal to her."

He picks me up and I wrap my arms around his neck. Pushing me against the wall, he slides his fingers over my panties. "You've got it, but we have to learn the art of sneaking around then."

His lips descend on mine and I immediately wonder why I fought this so hard, because the man can kiss like no other. His tongue does magical things in my mouth that I feel down to my core. He lowers my feet to the floor, then falls to his knees.

"I've been dying to taste you again all week." His hands venture up my dress. "Guess it's my lucky day since you wore a dress."

He hooks his fingers on either side of my panties and

drags them down my legs. My breath hitches when the air hits my clit, making it harden. Hooking one leg over his shoulder, he buries his face under the skirt of my dress.

My head falls to the wall with a thump at his breath blowing on my swollen lips. His finger trails back and forth and I know I'm soaked, anticipating the first swipe of his tongue.

I reach down to pull at his wet hair, anything I can grab, but all I get is my dress. I look down and the sight hits me like a lightning bolt, every nerve in my body standing on end. Somehow, it's almost more erotic that I can't *see* him, I can only feel what he's doing under my dress.

His tongue slides up my slit and rests on my clit, then he sucks it into his mouth. My eyes close and I grind along his face, needing more. He groans, one hand wrapping around me and squeezing my ass, pushing me into him harder.

"God, Gavin. I need more."

He must hear me because his free hand joins in, thrusting inside me. I raise up the wall, clenching around his finger, on my tiptoes each time he pushes his finger inside me, but he doesn't relent, adding another finger.

"Take it, baby. Whatever you need. Take it."

I ride his fingers as though they're his cock and he arches them to hit my G-spot, making me almost come on the spot, but I hold on, never wanting this feeling to stop. He twirls his tongue around my nub, eating me out as I grind against his face. The noises coming from his throat are enough to push me over the edge. My hands splay on either side of the wall, and it takes everything in me not to fall to the floor.

Just like last time, he places one sweet kiss on my core before coming out from under my dress. He rises up to tower over me and I pull him down to kiss me, tasting myself on his tongue. Again, he takes charge, picking me up and plopping me down on the desk before pulling a condom out of his pocket. He's inside me in seconds.

"Fuck, I'll never get tired of this. You're crazy if you think that." His mouth ravishes mine.

I feel the same way about Gavin. I'll never grow tired of having him deep inside me.

It's a done deal. Gavin Price has won me over.

Chapter Twenty-four

Gavin

It's been two weeks of sneaking around with Posey. I'm not really a fan of this whole secret relationship thing. I moved from LA to Sunrise Bay so I could get my morning coffee without cameras in my face. I'm trying to be understanding, but a night like tonight—when all I want to do is take her back to my house and forget about the shitty day—makes it more difficult.

Marla is doing better than me in the polls. I thought she might be. My mind has been occupied lately and I need to kick it into gear. So instead of being with Posey, I walk over to Truth or Dare Brewery to pick up my take-out order.

Cade is behind the bar and signals that he's got my order in the back when he sees me walk in.

While I'm waiting for him at the bar, Posey walks in with Mandi. I'm about to call her over, because we can pull off that we're kind of friendly. That wouldn't be suspicious at all. Yeah right. But I have no time before Eli Easton saunters up to her.

I watch him lean in and kiss her cheek. She smiles and they talk like the old friends I guess they are. There's no reason I should be jealous, but maybe it's because I want to be with Posey so badly, there's still insecurity there. I've been ridiculed for everything I've done my entire life, so I might suck at this boyfriend thing. Then again, I wouldn't know because she won't let us be public with our relationship.

Mandi leaves them to grab a seat and I groan. If she's with them, at least there's a buffer. Eli signals to a table of guys to his right. Posey leans forward and waves.

"You're just gonna stand there and watch?" Cade's voice surprises me and I jolt.

"Your sister can handle herself."

"Hey, Cade, can I get a Lucy Takes Flight? I can't decide what I want tonight." Mandi sits on the stool next to me. "What are we all looking at?"

"We're looking at Gavin allowing Eli Easton to try to win our sister over again."

I look at Mandi, who surely knows her sister better than Cade. "Don't you think that Posey will be pissed if I go over there all alpha male, pounding my chest like a Neanderthal?"

Mandi laughs. "Posey might pretend she doesn't like it."

Cade pours the different beers into the flight for Mandi, and I can't help but glance over my shoulder at Posey every second.

"Just go over there and put your arm around her," Mandi says.

"We're not a couple."

"Yeah, okkaaayy," Cade says. "This town isn't stupid. There have been reports all over about Posey and Gavin sightings. Here's a clue." Cade leans forward and lowers his voice. "Don't drive both cars to one place and then disappear on a 'hike.'" He uses air quotes.

Shit. We did that two days ago. My ass still has scratches from the pieces of wood on the ground. Neither of us thought to bring a blanket.

"Does Posey know about this?" I ask them.

"God no." Mandi sips her first beer. "If she did, then you'd be long gone. Don't worry, we all know how Posey is." She pats me on the back.

That's... worrisome.

I look over again and find Eli writing something down for Posey. Great, his fucking number, no doubt. "Why not tell her we've been outed?"

"I just told you, she'd break up with you and we know she doesn't want that." Mandi tries another beer.

My forehead creases. "Why would she break up with me?" This whole time, I thought, so what if we get outed because the hiding would be over. She'd have to come clean with everyone, including her mom.

"Has she not told you about our mom?" Mandi asks.

"And their relationship?" Cade adds.

As I'm about to pry for more information, Chevelle bounces over and kisses Mandi on the cheek. "Can I have a hard seltzer, the watermelon flavor one?"

Cade nods and heads over to the cooler. He cracks the bottle open for her, then heads down the other side of the bar to fulfill some orders.

Mandi turns to her sister. "Chevelle, what would happen if Posey found out people know about her and Gavin?"

She puts her finger over her throat and slides it across.

"I don't understand," I say. "We've had conversations. I know how important Marla is to her, but I also know how she feels about me."

Mandi and Chevelle look at one another.

"Mom is *everything* to her. She's Posey's one stable figure in her life. She'd give up everything for Mom." Mandi puts her hand on my forearm. "Including her own happiness."

Fuck. I blow out a breath. These aren't things I didn't know about or was worried about, but I didn't realize her mom was as big a stumbling block as she is. But I know I'm the cause of Posey's happiness, just as she is for me. I feel it when she's with me.

"I'll be right back." I push off the bar to go over to her.

"Take this. You won't be back." Chevelle holds up my food order.

I snatch it and weave through the weekend crowd over to Posey and Eli. Eli sees me first and I take some satisfaction in the fact that I can tell he's instantly pissed. It means he sees me as competition.

"Hey, you two," I say, placing my hand on the small of Posey's back.

She steps away and my hand drops.

"Gavin," Eli says without putting his hand out for me to shake.

That's fine. I wasn't going to be a gentleman either.

"Eli." I nod in his direction.

"Did you see Mandi? I came here with her?" Posey raises on her tiptoes to look over the crowd.

"Actually, I need to talk to you about the campaign." I turn to Eli. "Do you mind if I steal her away for a moment?"

Eli shakes his head. "I should get back to my friends. You have my number, Posey. Don't be afraid to use it."

I raise my eyebrows, trying not to get possessive right now.

"Yeah. Okay. See you, Eli."

Once she follows me outside, I walk over to my campaign headquarters and insert my key into the lock.

Inside, I toss my meal on my desk and push my hands through my hair. "I'm not sure how much longer I can do this."

"Do what?" She juts out her hip.

"I can't watch a guy flirt with you and do nothing about

it. Do you know how bad I wanted to slam you against that wall and kiss the living shit out of you right in front of him?"

She smiles as if this is a game. If it is, it's a game I want to end.

"I'm serious, Posey."

"I know." She walks toward me with a smirk that says she likes me all possessive, but I can't claim her until she allows us to be out in the open.

"I don't want to be a secret."

She steps up to me, chest to chest. "Take me home. To your house." Her finger trails down my front. "I'll make it up to you."

I take her hands. "This is more than sex for me."

She draws back and looks up at me. "Do you think that's all it is for me? Sex?"

"I'm trying to have a serious conversation and you're using your sex appeal to stop me from discussing it."

"I'm just making it up to you. I know this is hard and I promise—"

"I can't do it. I want to hold your hand in public. I want to kiss you whenever I want. I want Eli fucking Easton to know you're mine."

"But I am yours. Why do you have to prove that to anyone other than me?"

I sit in my chair. "I've never felt this way for someone, and I don't want to keep it a secret. I know you have your reasons, but I want to scream it from the rooftops."

She sits on my lap, wrapping her arms around my neck. "You do?"

"God, yes."

She kisses me. "This is really that important to you?"

I say nothing but raise my eyebrows.

She chuckles. "Just let me talk to my mom first, okay?"

"Yeah, that sounds familiar..."

"I promise. If I don't, you can have your way with me for an entire week."

I wrap my arms around her waist and pull her toward me. "Now I'm hard."

"Then take me home like I told you to."

I pat her on the ass to get her off my lap. Grabbing the bag of takeout, I take her hand and walk out the back of my office to my Bronco.

"GOD, GAVIN," she says breathlessly as I dip my head to lick up her neck. "I need you."

"I need you." I take her head in my hands and cover her mouth with mine. It's not just sex for me, but damn if the sex isn't spectacular. I situate myself between her legs— sadly, she's wearing jeans tonight. "Open for me."

"Take me to your bed." She grabs the hem of my shirt and pulls it off my body.

I pick her up, and she wraps her legs around my waist. While I climb the stairs, our mouths collide, tongues dueling for dominance. She's everything I've ever wanted and if Logan never would've told me about this town, I never would've met her.

I owe him big time.

I walk us through my bedroom door and drop her on the bed. She stares up at me and our eyes lock. She has no idea how gorgeous she is.

"Why are you up there when I'm down here?"

She takes hold of her T-shirt hem to pry it up, but I place my hands on hers, my knee on the bed and inching down to her. "That's my job."

She puts her arms out to either side. "Well then, what are you waiting for?"

My palms slide up under her T-shirt, grabbing her bra-covered tits.

She moans and squirms under me, her hands landing on either side of my head. "I'm yours, Gavin. All yours."

That's all it takes for me to lose all control. With frantic hands, we help one another get undressed and I grab a condom, rolling it down my length. Needing to claim her, if only here in this bedroom between the two of us.

I push into her with a hard thrust, but withdraw slowly. She gasps. Her red hair is splayed over my pillow and everything about this feels right. As if all the pieces to the puzzle of my life have been found and put in their proper place.

She matches my rhythm, synching our bodies as I move in and out of her, going a little deeper with every thrust. Everything around us slows and the only thing that matters is us. I watch her, the way her body bows off the mattress, offering all of herself to me.

I bring one of her legs up to lie along my torso and over my shoulder and push inside her, never getting deep enough. There's no playing it cool as inch by inch, moan by moan, we're each baring our hearts to the other. There's no hiding. She was meant for me and I for her.

"Harder," she moans.

I grind into her, and her fingernails dig into my biceps.

We lose ourselves in the beauty of our lovemaking.

"I'm yours," I whisper, and she sighs, her eyelids droopy with her impending orgasm.

"Yes," she pants.

"And you're mine?" I ask, knowing she's getting closer by the way her body is wiggling under me. With one hand, I massage her clit.

Her head thrashes side to side on the pillow. "Gavin," she says with a plea. "I'm yours. Forever."

She clenches around my length and her back arches off the bed for a moment before she tenses and falls back to the mattress. I continue to move in and out of her until my own orgasm rivals hers.

Afterward, she runs her hand down my cheek. Neither of us says a word because we know. Almost as if there was no choice about us, our story written by fate. We both know that tonight, what just happened transcended our relationship. All I can do is fall on top of her, lower her leg, and kiss her as if my life depends on it.

She's mine, and I'm hers.

Chapter Twenty-five

Posey

The smell of food wakes me, and I roll over to realize I'm in Gavin's warm bed. Grabbing his T-shirt, I throw it over my head and walk downstairs. His house is very nice, but I understand why he'd want to do some renovations. As I walk down the stairs, I hear him singing along to music.

Stopping right before I enter his kitchen, I rest my back along the wall and relish the moment. Last night wasn't our usual sex. Hiding our relationship has made the times we're together fast and furious because we're so thirsty for one another. But last night it felt like he was branding me, tattooing himself on me so I'd never be free of him.

As we were falling asleep, he whispered, "All yours," in my ear. I know he harbors some fears about being good enough, but he's more than enough.

I walk into the kitchen, and he looks up as he pours pancake batter into a pan. "There's the sleepyhead."

Without stopping, I go up to him and wrap my arms around his waist, then cast a series of kisses along his spine. "Good morning."

He covers my hands with his. "Good morning." Turning in my arms, he brushes back my wild mane of red hair. "Hungry?"

"Starving."

He leans back and grabs a napkin off a plate. "Sit and let me feed you."

I smile, eyeing the bacon, sausage, eggs, and pancakes.

"Since this is our first breakfast, I wasn't sure what you really liked."

"We had breakfast at Northern Lights," I say, rising on my tiptoes to kiss him.

"Powdered eggs don't count. I feel like I should go and cook for all of them so they get something decent as a thank you because without them, I'm not sure we would be here." He pulls out a fork and places it next to the plate.

While he finishes the pancakes, I pick at my prepared plate, not wanting to eat without him.

He flips the pancakes as though he's a short-order cook. "Are you available today?"

I nod. "Want to stay in bed all day?"

"Actually, I'd like us to get out of the house. I was thinking either we take a boat out or go on a hike." I open my mouth, but he holds up his hand. "I'm giving you a reprieve on outing us for a day because I just want to be with you today."

"It won't take long for me to tell my mom. Are you sure?"

He kisses me, then places the fork in my hand. "Yes, and eat before I feed you myself."

He pours us each a coffee and hands them to me. We sit at his breakfast area, him not eating much compared to my plate, but I'm not shy about eating when I'm hungry.

My phone rings in my purse. I stand and swivel around to get it, but he pulls me back into his lap.

"Can we forget the outside world for one day?"

I shift around and place my arm behind his head. "That sounds like heaven."

The call goes to my voice mail, and I wait to see if they left a message. They do, so I decide I'll check it after we eat breakfast.

I stay seated on Gavin's lap, feeding him some pancakes and eggs, the two of us sharing a fork. His fingers run light circles on my thighs. "A man could get used to this."

"I hope so."

He places a kiss on my neck, under my earlobe. "You're even more beautiful in the morning. That just-fucked look is an extreme turn-on for me."

I feel heat rush up my neck to my cheeks. "Okay, we need to get ready before we do end up spending all day in bed." I slide off his lap, pick up my dish, and take it to the sink. "We should clean up first."

He takes the plate out of my hand. "Go check your voice mail and meet me upstairs. I got this."

My shoulders fall and I look up at him.

"Do you think I don't already know that I won't have your full attention if you don't check your phone?" He chuckles.

I kiss his cheek. "You're one in a million."

I rush over to my phone. Searching for it in my purse, I finally feel it and pull it out.

Mom.

I rack my brain to make sure we didn't have any campaigning event that I didn't write down. Pressing on voice mail, I wait.

"Hey, sweetie, Hank and I were wondering if you could come over this afternoon for lunch. We're going to ask all the kids because... um... well, if you can't make it, just call. We're thinking around noon. Bye." She hangs up, and a sour feeling hits my stomach. I stand there for a bit going back over the call in my head.

Her voice was all shaky. I can tell she's hiding something.

"Who was it?" Gavin comes back in the kitchen, probably wondering why I didn't go upstairs. He's resting his arm on the doorframe, sipping his coffee.

"My mom."

Gavin holds the coffee cup at his side. "And?"

"She just called a family meeting. I mean, not in so many words, but that's what it is." My hands cover my stomach. "Something is wrong. I feel it in my gut."

He walks across the room and his hand covers mine. "It could be a wedding or baby announcement. Maybe they want to take you all on a vacation. Maybe they're selling the house."

I shake my head. "That's not the way this family works. We've had family meetings when my parents were divorcing, when we were moving up here, when she was marrying Hank, when they found out she was pregnant with Rylan... when big things are going to disrupt our lives." I lean my head on his shoulder. "It's bad, Gavin. I just know it."

He draws back and takes my chin in his hand. "Do you want me to come?"

I shake my head. "No. Not yet."

There's hurt in his eyes before he sets down his coffee and wraps me in his arms. "I'll be here when you're done, okay?"

I nod, pushing away the urge to call every sibling to see if they know what the hell is going on.

ALL OF MY siblings must've thought the same thing because we all show up at noon on the dot.

Cade and Presley are walking through the garage when I

pull up. Mandi and Chevelle are walking up the hill to the house. Jed and Molly don't have Emilia, which speaks volumes. Adam and Lucy pull up as I exit my car, and Fisher's truck is here, so I assume he and Allie are inside already.

It's the limo that pulls up that makes me stop before going into my parents' house.

Xavier exits and holds out his hand. Ugh. Giulia steps out of the limo.

"Makes me want to throw up," Chevelle says as she waits at the top of the driveway with me.

"I can't even watch it more than I have to." Mandi walks inside the house with Adam and Lucy after we all kiss hello and silently ask with our eyes if anyone knows what's going on.

"This is a family-only meeting," I say to Xavier, crossing my arms. I don't understand why he would bring his piece of eye candy.

Xavier doesn't let go of Giulia's hand. "Give me a break, we came back from Aruba for this."

"What?" My hands drop to my sides. It's definitely big if they called him home. "What's going on?"

"And what do you know?" Chevelle asks.

"I don't know anything. They called me two days ago and asked when I could get home. Here I am."

"It was raining anyway," Giulia snipes.

Logan and Nikki walk up the driveway, sans Noah.

"So sorry we're cutting into your margarita time," Chevelle says sarcastically, and we both turn around to head into the house.

I stop when I see that chairs have been brought into the family room. The hairs on my neck rise. Usually, it's a free-for-all. You get here early, you get a seat. If not, you're on the floor.

Hank is sitting in his favorite chair, and other than him being in pajama pants and a San Francisco Rebels sweatshirt, nothing is unusual. He doesn't look pale or sick. Mom is trying to serve everyone drinks, and she even has snacks out on the coffee table that Xavier's helping himself to.

"Just sit down, Marla," Hank says in a sterner voice than he usually uses with my mom.

She sits next to Allie, who is holding Axel. For the first time ever, probably, Mom doesn't ask to hold him. Allie and I share a look across the room.

"I'm so sorry I'm late." A voice comes from the hallway, and we all look around the room because everyone is here. But then Clara comes to the doorway and stops.

"I thought this was family only?" Xavier says in the same tone I used outside.

"Well, your girl toy is here," Chevelle sneers.

"I invited Clara. She's family." Marla waves her in. "Have a seat, sweetie."

Cade gets up so Clara can sit next to Presley.

"Just tell us," Jed blurts.

Mom looks at Hank. Obviously they didn't discuss which of them should tell us.

Hank clears his throat. "As you know, I haven't been feeling great. I've gone to the doctor, and we didn't want to worry any of you, so we wanted to make sure all the tests were done before we talked to you."

Tension fills the room as if someone just pulled a pin from a grenade. I hold my breath.

"I want to preface this by saying that I'm good and I'm going to be fine."

"Where's Grandma? Why isn't she here?" Adam asks.

"Grandma's already been told," Hank says.

We all look at one another.

"Back to me." Hank points at himself. "I'm sick, and I'm going to have to have surgery and some radiation."

"Cancer?" Cade asks in a whisper.

Hank turns to his oldest son and nods.

It's like the floor drops out from under me. I picture what my mom was like when she left my dad and know she'd be a thousand times worse if she lost Hank.

"Prostate cancer, which is a highly treatable form of cancer," Mom says and pats Hank's knee. "He's going to get through this. You don't have to worry."

"But... I don't..." Xavier sputters. "Did they catch it early then?"

The quietness in a room that's usually filled with chaos when we're all together feels alien and tells everyone how serious this is. There's a good chance he'll be fine, that he'll come out on the other side all right. But I'm not naive enough to think it's a guarantee. There's a family out there somewhere whose doctor told them they'd beat it and they didn't. There are too many what-ifs.

"What can we do?" Mandi asks.

"A meal train," Nikki says.

"We can all take turns visiting Dad. Taking him to radiation and back."

Everyone throws out fix-it ideas and Mom addresses each one. All of us want to take the burden off of Mom, pitch in and help where we can.

"No!" Hank yells into the fray.

All the commotion stops, and we look at Hank.

"We don't need anyone's help. I'll be fine. I am fine. You continue on with your lives. I've told Marla to continue with the mayoral race, and I want each and every one of you to do the same. Presley doesn't need to be making me any meals while she's eight months pregnant or being around me after I've had radiation. My grandchildren will not see me weak." He stands and leaves the room.

My mom drops her head and covers her face with her hands for a moment before standing. "Excuse me, everyone. Just give me a moment."

I rise from my chair and follow my mom.

"Posey, maybe you should give her a sec," Nikki says.

"Why? She should know she's not in this alone."

Nikki blows out a breath, and I leave my siblings to make sure my mom is okay.

I find her in the living room, and I grab a box of tissues, passing one to her. "It'll be okay."

She nods, blotting her eyes. "I know, but I need to tell you something." She looks up and her eyes are red-rimmed with tears still streaking down her cheeks. "I'm taking myself out of the race."

"But Hank said—"

She shakes her head. "Sweetie, Hank is way more important than being mayor. All of you are. My family comes first. Gavin will make a good mayor." She pats my knee.

"But..."

She inhales deeply. "Thank you for all your help. I've had a lot of fun with you these weeks." She pats my knee, stands, and leaves the room.

That's it. She's just going to give up on her own happiness. Well, I'm not.

Chapter Twenty-six

Gavin

A knock sounds on my door and I open it to find Posey there. She rushes into my arms, tears spilling from her eyes.

"Whoa, baby, are you okay?" Fuck, I had high hopes that it was good news. One of her siblings having a baby or maybe an anniversary trip or something.

"Hank..." She wails and her tears wet my shirt.

"Hank what?" I rub her back.

She pulls away and wipes her eyes. "He's sick. Cancer."

My stomach drops. "Fuck," I say, running a hand through my hair.

She walks into the kitchen and opens the fridge. I follow her.

"Prostate. They say he's going to be okay, but no one can guarantee that." She turns to me. "Do you have any alcohol here?"

I raise my eyebrows.

"Shit. Sorry, stupid question."

"We can go out if you want?" I'm not a fan of covering up your feelings with alcohol, but I have to remember that others can manage it better than I ever could.

"No, it's fine. My mom is going to pull herself from the election."

From her tone, I gather that she's pissed. "Why would she do that?"

It feels weird to ask, given that I'll be the benefactor if she does.

She shakes her head. "I mean, I understand. Hank is sick, and it's horrible and I'm upset too. But this is something she's wanted for a long time."

"Maybe she feels like her attention needs to be on Hank right now."

She glares at me. "There are enough of us that it's not necessary. She's sacrificing her own happiness when we can all help out."

Shit, I didn't see that coming. "Don't you think Hank *is* her happiness?"

She shoots me a glare. "I know that. Hank's her life, but last time she let a man get in the way of her happiness, he left her. What if...?"

"What if what?" Please tell me she isn't going where I think she is.

"Things don't always go as planned. What if something happens to Hank and then she just gave up and she's left with nothing again?"

Okay, we're going down this road.

I take her hand and lead her to the other room, where I sit her down on the couch. "Posey, take a deep breath."

She does. At least half a breath anyway.

"These are things you can't control."

"No. I can." She pokes me in the chest, standing. "I was thinking on the way over here. I can run for mayor. Then when Hank is healthy again, I'll just step down and she can take my place."

I lean forward and rest my forearms on my knees. "Are you serious?"

"Isn't it brilliant? Then she's not giving up anything."

"And you're so sure you'll win?"

I'm not even sure she's thinking rationally right now. Her head is swamped with thoughts of possibly losing her second father.

"I'm a Greene," she says. "Of course."

I push myself off the couch. "And me? Where do I fit into your master plan?"

She stops for a moment and finally the light bulb goes on that her royal plan has a snag in it. "Well... I'll hire you. So you can still get everything you want, and everyone wins."

I'm at a loss for words. Watching her in this almost manic state, as though she's a nurse in a war zone, trying to fix everyone's wounds, is unsettling. She's not fixing anything really; she's just putting Band-Aids over gushing wounds.

"I want to be mayor. I've made that clear."

She puts her hands on her hips. "So what? You want my mom to just withdraw and let you win by default?"

I throw my hands in the air. "I don't want your mom to withdraw, but if she feels like she should, then I can't stop her. What I'm upset about is that you're going to throw your hat in."

Her face scrunches in apparent confusion. "Why?"

"You seriously don't see a problem with this? I don't want to sound selfish, but whose happiness is more important?" I raise my hand. "Forget I asked that. I don't want to know."

I have to get out of here before I say something I can't take back.

"You know what? Do what you want." I walk up the

stairs and grab one of the suitcases I keep stored under my bed.

Her footsteps sound on each step as she comes up after me. To think that this morning, I watched her sleep and pictured our life together. I shake my head as I toss the suitcase on the bed. I've been tricked into thinking I'm as important to her as she is to me.

"Are you going somewhere?" Her voice is weak and distant.

"Back to LA. I have things to take care of down there anyway and I really need some time to think things over."

"What?" Her voice raises an octave. "Was this all a game to you? Get me close and leave?"

I abandon my suitcase. "No actually. I was gonna ask you to come with me for a weekend. But you have your own priorities. Plus, you should stick around if you're gonna replace your mom on the ballot."

"You're really that mad?"

I grab my underwear and toss it in my bag, then my shorts and T-shirts. "Yes, if you hadn't noticed, I am."

"I don't understand why."

"Because you're going to sabotage my happiness. Do you not see that? You know the mayoral race is important to me."

"But my mom..."

I point at her. "I like your mom. She's a great woman, but she's a grown woman who knows what she wants, and right now she wants to be with her husband. I think that's admirable. She can make the decision for herself. But now you're making decisions that affect me and work against my happiness. If I won, I wanted to win fair and square. I'll feel undeserving winning by default anyway, but there's clearly a disconnect between me and you."

She sits on the edge of the bed, staring into the suitcase I'm packing. "That's it?"

"Yeah. That's it. You obviously don't see the problem and I'm not going to try to explain it again." I pick up my suitcase and walk down the stairs. Anything else I can pick up in LA. "Lock up if that's not too much trouble. God forbid someone sees you at my house."

I slam the front door and climb into my Bronco.

She pulls open the front door. "You son of a bitch. You played me!"

I roll down the window. "If you honestly believe that, then we're definitely over."

I speed off down the road by the bay, eager to get out of here. This small town has never felt so small. I only make it to the stop sign before I rest my forehead on the steering wheel. What the hell just happened?

My tires squeal on the pavement as I take off. I need to make one more stop before heading to the airport.

I WALK UP the walkway of Marla and Hank's house, not even sure what I'm about to say. There are still a few trucks here that I know belong to Posey's siblings. I ring the doorbell and step back so there's some room.

Marla opens the door, her head tilted in apparent confusion. "Gavin."

"Hi, Marla. Posey told me about Hank, and I wanted to say that I'm really sorry. He, as well as your entire family, will be in my thoughts."

"She just left. Did she go straight to you?" Her eyes crinkle as if she doesn't understand. Maybe Mandi and

Chevelle were wrong. Maybe everyone doesn't know about us.

I nod. "She did."

"Oh. I had no idea you two had grown that close."

I take a deep breath. "I really care for your daughter. A lot. And until just now, I thought she cared... you know what? That doesn't matter. I just wanted to let you know that you've been nothing but gracious to me since I moved here. I never went into my decision to run against you lightly. I'm not even sure I expected to win."

"Gavin." She opens the door wider. "Would you like to come in?"

I shake my head. "No, thank you. I'm almost done. Anyway, I just want to say I'm sorry this horrible thing is happening to two nice people like you and Hank. But I've learned life is unfair and cruel and doesn't punish the ones who should be."

"Please, Gavin, come in." She opens up the door farther.

I shake my head adamantly. "Posey is at my house right now. She's going to be upset. I think... I think we just broke up. I have to go to LA and sort some things out. Just... can you send someone to make sure she's okay?"

She looks behind her, steps on the porch, and shuts the door. "I know I'm not your mom, but I'm going to tell you what I would tell my boys. Do *not* run away. Whatever happened is not unfixable. Posey is... she can have a one-track mind. I can see that whatever transpired, she's hurt you. Just give her an hour and I swear she'll see the error of her ways."

"I can't. I'm sorry. Just please send someone to check on her. And I'll be thinking only good things about Hank's health. Hopefully this is just a blip in the road."

She offers me a sweet smile. But instead of asking me to stay again, she nods that she understands.

I walk down the path back to my truck, slide in, and pull out of her driveway. The entire way to the airport, I deny the urge to turn my truck around. I've played second to everyone else's desires my entire life and I can't allow myself to accept that position in the life of the woman I love.

Chapter Twenty-seven

Posey

I take the keys from the front table and lock Gavin's door. Not knowing what to do with the key, I figure I'll hold on to it until he returns. Logan can pass it on to him or something.

An SUV pulls down the path and stops, and I recognize it as my mom's. She gets out and leans against the vehicle.

"How did you know I was here?"

"A little six-foot-tall birdie told me," she says and pushes off her small SUV, walking toward me.

I drop down on the front stoop of his house, settling my purse between my legs. "What else did he tell you?"

She joins me on the stairs. "Something I probably should have heard from you. It's okay, you know."

"What gave it away?" I ask.

"When he showed up with Erwin for the hair class." She chuckles. "But I think I saw it in both your eyes when you'd look at each other. You tried really hard not to like one another, but I could tell." She sits next to me and hits her shoulder to mine.

"Well, it's over now."

"I heard. Want to fill in the blanks for me?"

I turn to my mom. "I disregarded his happiness."

"Is this about the mayoral race? What did you do, Posey?"

I swear this woman always knows when I did something bad.

"I can't ever take it back."

"Oh, I don't believe that." She looks at me, waiting for me to tell her.

"I told him I was going to run in your place so that when Hank is all healthy, I can step down and you can be mayor."

My mom blows out a long breath. "And where did he fit in this new equation?"

"That's what he wanted to know. I said I'd hire him."

She nods and a small noise escapes to confirm that I might've blown it. "You know, I probably should've addressed this with you a long time ago. Each of you harbors such different scars from your dad's and my divorce. You've always thought it was your job to make me happy. But there are a few things you probably don't know."

My forehead wrinkles. "What?"

"First, I enjoyed my years at home with you. I wouldn't have swapped those out for a career even if I'd known your dad and I would divorce. I loved being the room mom, volunteering, and hearing about your day when I'd pick you up from school. Those are things that not all moms get and I'm grateful for them. I treasure those memories. Yes, it made it more difficult when your dad and I divorced. Especially when we argued about Jed. But I wouldn't change a thing. And I love my salad dressing company, but I think I really loved it the most when you guys would all come and help me with a big order. My family is my happy place, Posey."

"But you wanted to be mayor?"

She rests her hand on my knee. "I did. Because Rylan

doesn't need me like he did, and Hank is working a lot. I figured since the majority of my kids run businesses in Sunrise Bay, I'd be able to see them. That's not the only reason, but when we heard Hank was sick, none of that mattered to me. The only thing that mattered was more time with him. Believe me, Hank and I have already fought over this enough. I don't need to fight over it with you too." She pats my leg. "It's time you find your own happiness, and that can't be making me happy. I should've never allowed you to be my campaign manager. That was my mistake."

"I wanted to be," I insist.

I rest my head on her shoulder and she wraps her arm around me. "I know, sweetie, but I think you're denying yourself a pretty great opportunity if you let that man get on a plane."

"I blew it, Mom." Admitting it out loud feels like a knife in the ribs.

"You didn't blow it. That boy showed up on my doorstep to make sure someone came over here to check on you. A man who is checked out of a relationship doesn't do that. God knows your father..." She kisses the top of my head. "Never mind. We're not going to go there." She pushes lightly and nudges me back. "Do you love him? Be honest."

Tears well in my eyes and streak down my face. I nod.

"Say it, Posey, own it."

"I do. I love him, Mom. He's different than any other boy. He's so sweet to me and treats me like I'm special." More tears tumble down, and I lose control. "And I hurt him. I didn't put his happiness above everyone else's. He kept giving me a chance to fix my mistake, and I just kept going on like a robot or something. Not understanding..." I sniffle and wipe my nose. "He has his own insecurities, and I disregarded all that. He's too good for me."

She laughs.

"What?"

"I thought the same thing about Hank. But the truth is, we're easy to love." She knocks our foreheads together. "In all seriousness, this will not be the first fight you have. You guys aren't even public yet. All you can do is apologize and see if he'll take you back."

"I'm scared though."

She nods. "You've never put yourself out there, Posey. But I think this guy might be worth having all of you, and maybe it's mother's intuition, but I think he can handle it. He'll take good care of you, but you have to trust him. He's not your father, sweetie. Don't let your dad's decisions dictate your future. Life is too short. Hank being sick brings that front and center. Take the opportunities, don't squander them."

I hug her, squeezing her so tightly. "Thank you so much. I love you."

She squeezes me back.

"Okay, I'm going to try to catch him. Do you know which airport? Anchorage, I assume. I doubt he had a flight already booked." I scramble down the walkway but have to go back to get my purse. "I'm going. Wish me luck."

"Good luck," my mom says.

I climb into my car and speed down the street, praying he'll take me back. He's living his second chance after rehab. Hopefully he'll let me have my own.

I ARRIVE at Anchorage airport an hour later with little hope that he's still here. Regardless, I have to look for him to be sure.

"Posey," Xavier says when I walk into the check-in area.

"You just come into town and leave? Nice." I have no patience right now for Xavier and his new "I'm cooler than you" attitude.

"I think you'll want to be nice to me." He crosses his arms.

"Where is Giulia?"

"Bathroom. Come. Follow me."

I look up at the departures to find the ones going to LA. Then it dawns on me. I have to figure a way to get farther into the terminal. Even more than that, Gavin might be flying private.

"How did you get here?" I ask my stepbrother.

"Private." He's so smug I want to punch him.

"Can you get me to the terminals? I just have to check the flights."

"For Gavin?" he asks, his arrogance stinging with his know-it-all raised eyebrows.

"Spit it out, X," I say. "Where is he?"

"Are you going to be nice to me?"

"Fine."

"Follow me."

I follow Xavier through security, where he shows passes that we're flying private.

"He stopped by the house. I guess he and Giulia have a past. She wants to fly home, and she volunteered for him to use the private jet, so I'm just here to see them off. I'm going to stay for a while with Dad." He glances over his shoulder. "I'm not the asshole you take me for. Family is still very important to me."

"What about Clara?" I should be nicer to him, since he's doing me a favor.

"That's between us." His voice is void of emotion.

We walk down a corridor, and there sits Gavin with his head in his hands. Giulia has her hand on his back, rubbing small circles.

Xavier says, "The man is a mess. Should I kick his ass? Did he hurt you?"

I shake my head. "I hurt him."

"Well, now's your chance to fix it. I know how you love fixing things." Xavier holds out his arm for me to lead the way.

I tentatively walk forward. "Gavin?"

His head lifts and he soaks me in. The hurt is clear in his eyes, but so is his love.

"Can we talk?" I ask.

Giulia steps away and I take her seat.

"How do you know her?" Then I shake my head, not wanting to know. "Never mind. Not my business."

"We dated. Years ago. Nothing serious."

"You don't have to be truthful all the time. I'd rather not see who I need to compare myself to." I let out a nervous laugh, but he doesn't laugh at all.

Gavin keeps his eyes on the floor between his legs. I can't do this without his eyes on mine, so I slide off the seat and kneel between his legs.

"I'm so sorry. I'm an idiot. I was blinded by the fact that we could lose Hank and if we did, how would my mom ever recover from that? He's her whole world. So I went into fix-it mode. How could I prepare ahead of time so that she'd be able to pick herself up? And I..."

He lifts his head and inhales a deep breath. "I know why you did it." His voice is rough. "But I can't do the secrets anymore. I'm sorry if your mom talked to you, but I couldn't leave you crying and not have someone be there for you."

I shake my head. "I don't care about that. Not at all. I

want everyone to know that we're a couple. I want to hold your hand in public. And kiss you."

"This is a one-eighty." A nervous laugh escapes him.

"I mean it. I finally realized that I can't control my mom's happiness. Only my own happiness. And you make me happy. So happy." A tear slips out.

He reaches up and swipes it away. "I'm not sure, Posey."

"It's time to board," a woman comes over and says to Xavier.

"Give them one minute," he says.

"We cannot be delayed. We have our take-off time and the aircraft is waiting."

Gavin stands and I slide out of his way, using the chair next to him to stand. He steps forward and kisses my forehead. "We can talk about it."

Then he walks away and my heart caves in on itself. Talk about it whenever he returns, he means.

He turns around and holds his hand out to me. "On the plane."

"Now? You want me to go now?" My mouth hangs open.

"The decision is yours." He smiles. I eagerly take his hand and he pulls me to him. "Good decision."

I laugh, but his mouth descends on mine, swallowing my laughter.

He closes the kiss and runs his thumb back and forth on my cheek. "I just have one question."

"Yes?"

"Who are you going to vote for?" He smiles and my stomach flips.

"Technically I don't have to share my vote with anyone."

He pulls me tighter and buries his head close to my ear. "Say it, baby," he whispers.

"Price," I whisper. "I vote for you."

"Then let's get on this plane so I can thank you properly for your vote." He places a chaste kiss on my forehead.

"Does this mean I get to join the mile high club?" I ask.

Xavier groans from behind me, and Gavin laughs.

"I'm not sure Guilia would like that." He kisses me again. "I love you, Posey Greene."

My heart swells until it feels as if it might burst out of my chest. "And I love you, Gavin Price."

He kisses me and takes my hand, leading me to our happily ever after.

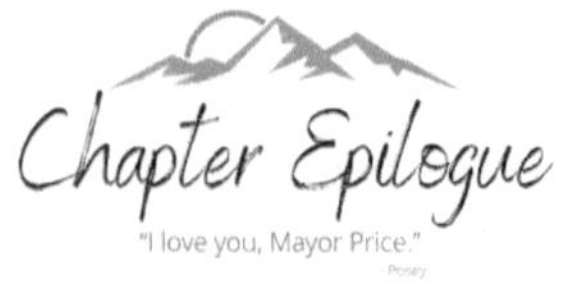

Posey

Election Day

Although we know that Gavin won the election since he's the only one running, he's still there at the voting booth, passing out stickers and thanking people for voting.

I walk in dressed in a sundress and sandals, my purse swung over my shoulder. He's talking to George Lehmann about a place to put a Vietnam War Memorial. The Gossip Brigade told Gavin they knew about us well before we outed ourselves and maybe since they scratched his back, he could scratch his. He's starting to realize how small-town politics work.

Gavin catches sight of me over George's shoulder, his gaze following me to the check-in desk. I wait my turn to cast my vote, feeling his smoldering gaze on me the entire time.

"I'll bring it up at the first meeting, George. You have my word." He shakes George's hand.

"Okay, just remember you might not be with her if it weren't for us," George says and eyes me when he leaves. "Posey."

I nod. "Mr. Lehmann."

"Thank you for coming in and voting today," Gavin says, standing right next to me. "I'm sure someone as beautiful as you has a lot of other things to do."

"Do you flirt with all the voters?" I ask in a sweet voice I rarely use.

Even Gavin can't get the smirk off his face. "Oh, I'm just friendly."

"Then could you kindly stop looking down my blouse?" I put my hand up to cover it even though I undid one button right before I stepped in.

Hey, we're keeping the magic alive.

"Sorry. I can't help myself." He grins.

"I thought I heard you had an amazing girlfriend," I say.

"I do. She might be into the whole threesome thing though."

I look at him and lift my eyebrows. He chuckles.

"Sorry, I'm planning this celebration nightcap for my boyfriend. After I vote, I have to jet to the store to make myself into a sundae."

He growls and clears his throat. "Sundae?"

"You know. Chocolate sauce, caramel, whipped cream."

He runs his hand over his forehead and his breathing hitches. "Cherries. Don't forget the cherries."

I giggle, unable to keep the charade going. "Never. He loves cherries. And ice. Likes to take an ice cube..." I lower my voice. "He places it in his mouth and glides it along my nipple. Drives me crazy."

"Is that so? I guess I'll be sure to try that on my girlfriend."

"You should."

A booth becomes available.

"Well, anything you want me to know before I go in there and cast my vote?" I look around.

A few people are checking in, but they probably assume Gavin and I are talking about what to do tonight for dinner or something since I moved into his house last week. We zoomed right over that whole proper date thing.

"Well." He leans in close to my ear, his hand molding to my hip. "I have a seven-inch cock and know exactly how to use it."

My face heats and I push him lightly. "Now that's playing dirty, Mr. Price."

"The sundae thing was playing dirty. I've got to get through two more hours here with a raging hard-on."

I laugh and walk backward toward my voting booth. "I'm going to go vote now."

He mouths, "I love you," and my heart pitter-patters. God, that man.

I can barely focus in the booth. When I exit, he's talking to someone else a few feet away and his hands are stuffed in his pockets, but I swear he adjusts himself when I give him a wave and a wink.

"Have fun at the store, baby," Gavin says.

"Do you need anything?" I ask.

"Not that I can think of. I think your list was detailed enough."

I slide my tongue along my bottom lip.

"Posey," Erwin says, playing with his Rubik's Cube near the entryway. Gavin didn't feel right telling on Midge, so he bought another one for Erwin, which made him happy, even if it wasn't his original one.

Later that night, I have everything ready to turn myself into Gavin's celebratory sundae, but the doorbell rings right when I thought he'd be home. We'd decided on no party, that we would wait up all night and see him win together.

I open the door, see who's there, and shut the door again.

Mandi bangs on the door. "Open up, Posey!"

I peek through the opening. "Sorry, Posey isn't home."

But Mandi and Chevelle use their weight to open the door. In walks my entire family, carrying plates of food. Everyone from the twins to Lucy and Adam's new foster child, Trey. He's about Emilia's age and they're inseparable every time we're together.

"Did you honestly think you were going to get away without having a party?" Cade shakes his head. "Where is the new mayor anyway?"

"On his way, I presume."

"Posey!" Mom hollers from the kitchen. "Why do you need all these cherries? Are you making a pineapple upside down cake? If you are, you only need about fifteen maybe."

"Cherry! Cherry!" Emilia yells and I hear the snap of the bottle being opened. Okay then.

Hank smiles at me. "I can't wait to tell Gavin he's got me to thank for being mayor. Your mom would've beat his ass."

I laugh. "I know." I don't really. Gavin has wormed his way into a lot of people's hearts, not just mine, in his short time here. "How are you feeling?"

"A lot better if people would stop asking me that question." His surgery is planned for next week and he'll start radiation right away. He kisses my cheek. "You look happy."

"Where's Gia?" Nikki asks Xavier.

"Giulia," he corrects her.

She shrugs. "Same difference."

"No, it's not the same. Is your name Natalie?"

Xavier hasn't left to go back to San Francisco yet. But so far, I haven't seen him with Clara, which upsets everyone in the family. He and Clara were best friends, and all I can assume is that something horrible happened to make this chasm between them so deep.

"Whatever. Does the ego need inflating again now that you've been back home for a bit?" Leave it to Nikki to put it all out there.

"You know what, Nikki? Who cares if I'm dating a model and I like my life in San Francisco? I can go into any restaurant and get seated, no reservations needed. People know me when I walk around the city and I like the finer things in life. So what?"

Nikki fakes excitement as though she's really impressed. "Logan can do the same in Las Vegas. Gavin can do it in Los Angeles. Do they do it? No."

"Noah's crying and Emilia's trying to give him a cherry," Mandi says to Nikki. After Nikki rushes into the other room, Mandi looks at Xavier. "You can thank me later."

The front door opens and we all quiet.

"Baby, I'm home and I've been thinking about my cherries," Gavin calls.

I run to the foyer and shake my head. "Did you not see all the cars outside?"

He glances toward the front door. "No."

I go past him and open the door. Sure enough, it's empty. "Okay, I'm so confused."

"Surprise!" Emilia screams when she sees Gavin. "It was supposed to be a surprise. You ruined the surprise, Aunt Posey."

"No one told me it was a surprise. I didn't even know they were coming," I tell Gavin.

"Does Emilia have my cherries on her fingers?" Gavin watches Emilia like a vulture, ready to descend and grab them.

Emilia plucks one off her finger and chews it. Trey follows her with more cherries.

Gavin growls.

"Relax, I bought two jars." I kiss his cheek. "And I'll stay up all night to make you your sundae."

His hands fall to my ass, and he squeezes. "You better."

The door creaks open and Clara pokes her head in. "Oh, I missed the surprise."

"No, you didn't. No one told me it was a surprise." I smile at her.

She laughs. "Classic." She holds out a dish. "Where do you want it?"

"In the kitchen." I thumb in that direction.

"Congratulations, Gavin," Clara says. "For more than just your mayor position." She winks and disappears around the corner.

"All I want is you right now," Gavin whines.

I wrap my arms around his shoulders and rise up on my tiptoes. "I know, but these people are part of the package that comes with me."

"I know. Let's go." He smacks me on the ass.

We walk into the main family room, and everyone roars with congratulations as though they didn't know he was home. As Gavin makes his way around the room, shaking hands and thanking everyone—something he'll be doing for some time—I keep my eyes on Xavier and Clara. Especially when Xavier takes Clara's hand, and she lets him lead her into the now empty dining room.

"Oh shit," Chevelle says behind me, and we both inch toward the room to overhear.

"Just talk to me," Xavier says.

"Why? You don't own me."

"I thought I was doing what was right."

"Where is Giulia?" she asks.

"She's in Milan."

"I think it's great that you're here for your dad, X, but as far as me and you? Just keep on walking when you see me. You can have your model girlfriend lick your wounds after a bad game now."

She turns to leave and Chevelle and I move fast, our backs straight along the wall.

"We've been best friends our entire lives," Xavier says, but I can't see his face.

"Past tense. We *were* best friends. You chose to ruin everything."

"I did not," he says, sounding pissed.

"Just stay out of my way while you're in Sunrise Bay." She walks out of the room and walks right by us, probably knowing we were listening.

Chevelle and I pretend to be in a deep conversation when Xavier comes out. He blows out his breath and walks out the front door to the porch. Chevelle and I share a look.

"Are we ever going to find out what happened?" I ask.

"Let's go corner Presley. Surely with her being ready to pop, she's hormonal. She'll be at a disadvantage." Chevelle drags me, but we're stopped by Cam's big body sliding in front of her.

"Stop being nosy."

Chevelle tries to go around him. "You might be my boss at work but not here."

His nostrils flare and I just mosey on away.

Grandma Ethel and Dori are sitting on the couch, being a little too quiet. Never a good sign.

My family stays the entire night until it's officially announced that Gavin won the election.

After everyone finally leaves, Gavin comes out of the kitchen with two empty cherry bottles.

I give him a pitying look. "I'll buy more tomorrow."

"It's okay. I want you in something else tonight."

I wait for him to say what, but instead, he sets the empty cherry bottles on the end table, then pulls a large-ish box from behind his back.

"Shouldn't I be the one getting you a gift?" I ask.

"It kind of is for me."

"Oh, I like the sound of that." I open the box to find a nightgown similar to Midge's, but it's new with tags on it.

"I know how much you loved it and I've been working for weeks to track one down. I found a woman who actually makes nightgowns in this style."

"So, no fertility nightgown?" I ask to clarify.

He chuckles. "No. But... if you..."

I shake my head, taking his hand and leading him to the couch. I straddle him and place my hand on his gorgeous face. Who would've ever thought all those years ago that my celebrity crush would fall in love with me? "Just you and me for a bit."

His arms tighten around me. "I'm on board with that."

"Good. Now take me to our bed."

"Anything you want, baby."

"I love you, Mayor Price," I whisper as he climbs the stairs with my legs wrapped around him.

"Music to my fucking ears."

He kicks the bedroom door shut and locks it. Just in case. You never know with my family.

The End

ALSO BY PIPER RAYNE

The Baileys

Lessons from a One-Night Stand (FREE)

Advice from a Jilted Bride

Birth of a Baby Daddy

Operation Bailey Wedding (Novella)

Falling for My Brother's Best Friend

Demise of a Self-Centered Playboy

Confessions of a Naughty Nanny

Operation Bailey Babies (Novella)

Secrets of the World's Worst Matchmaker

Winning my Best Friend's Girl

Rules for Dating Your Ex

Operation Bailey Birthday (Novella)

The Greene Family

My Twist of Fortune (Free Prequel)

My Beautiful Neighbor (FREE)

My Almost Ex

My Vegas Groom

A Greene Family Summer Bash (Novella)

My Sister's Flirty Friend

My Unexpected Surprise

My Famous Frenemy

A Greene Family Vacation (Novella)

My Scorned Best Friend

My Fake Fiancé

My Brother's Forbidden Friend

A Greene Family Christmas (Novella)

Lake Starlight

The Problem with Second Chances

The Issue with Bad Boy Roommates

The Trouble with Runaway Brides

The Drawback of Single Dads

Plain Daisy Ranch

One Last Summer

The One I Left Behind

The One I Stood Beside

The One I Didn't See Coming

Modern Love

Charmed by the Bartender

Hooked by the Boxer

Mad about the Banker

Single Dads Club

Real Deal

Dirty Talker

Sexy Beast

Hollywood Hearts

Mister Mom

Animal Attraction

Domestic Bliss

Bedroom Games

Cold as Ice

On Thin Ice

Break the Ice

Chicago Law

Smitten with the Best Man

Tempted by my Ex-Husband

Seduced by my Ex's Divorce Attorney

Blue Collar Brothers

Flirting with Fire

Crushing on the Cop

Engaged to the EMT

White Collar Brothers

Sexy Filthy Boss

Dirty Flirty Enemy

Wild Steamy Hook-up

The Rooftop Crew

My Bestie's Ex

A Royal Mistake

The Rival Roomies

Our Star-Crossed Kiss

The Do-Over

A Co-Workers Crush

Hockey Hotties

Countdown to a Kiss (Free Prequel)

My Lucky #13 (FREE)

The Trouble with #9

Faking it with #41

Tropical Hat Trick (Novella)

Sneaking around with #34

Second Shot with #76

Offside with #55

Kingsmen Football Stars

False Start (Free Prequel)

You Had Your Chance, Lee Burrows

You Can't Kiss the Nanny, Brady Banks

Over My Brother's Dead Body, Chase Andrews

Chicago Grizzlies

On the Defense (Free Prequel)

Something like Hate

Something like Lust

Something like Love

The Nest

Mr. Heartbreaker

Mr. Broody

Mr. S (Title to be revealed)

Mr. C (Title to be revealed)

Holiday Romances

Single and Ready to Jingle

Claus and Effect

Merry Kissmas

COCKAMAMIE UNICORN RAMBLINGS

Hold on why we pat ourselves on our backs for actually doing what we originally planned when it came to this story. We brought Gavin in way back in book three, My Vegas Groom, knowing he was Posey's hero.

We will admit, the mayoral election thing did take some figuring out which is why Sam Klein decided to stick around for another term. All in all, it all worked out in the end.

This was one of our chug, chug, chug books. We had a lot going on in our lives personally that had us pushing our deadline, not only once but twice. In the end once it was finished, we loved the underlying sexual tension between all their banter.

Unfortunately, there isn't anything that changed dramatically from plotting to page for us to talk about. Don't worry, the next book our ramblings will be three pages deep with changes. lol

As always, we have a lot of people to thank for getting this book into your hands...

Danielle Sanchez and the entire Wildfire Marketing Solutions team.
Cassie from Joy Editing for line edits.

Ellie from My Brother's Editor for line edits.

Rosa from My Brother's Editor for proofreading.

Hang Le for the cover and branding for the entire series.

Wander Aguiar for his awesome job of photographing our Posey and Gavin. It portrays their sweet story.

Bloggers who consistently carve out time to read, review and/or promote us.

Piper Rayne Unicorns who are our safe place in this crazy world!

Readers who took the time to read our story when there's so many choices out there. We are grateful beyond words for your support!

Next up is the couple a lot of you have been waiting for. Talk about teasing out a couple from book one! My Scorned Best Friend is next, but first you'll get the novella Greene Family Vacation where yes, we're sure to give you more teasing on Clara and Xavier. ;)

xo,

Piper & Rayne

ABOUT PIPER & RAYNE

Piper Rayne is a USA Today Bestselling Author duo who write "heartwarming humor with a side of sizzle" about families, whether that be blood or found. They both have e-readers full of one-clickable books, they're married to husbands who drive them to drink, and they're both chauffeurs to their kids. Most of all, they love hot heroes and quirky heroines who make them laugh, and they hope you do, too!